TYREAN MARTINSON

NEUS

RAYATANA, BOOK 2

Copyright © 2020 by Tyrean Martinson

NEXUS

The Rayatana Series, Book Two

All rights reserved. Except as permitted under the U.S. Copyright Act of 1976, no part of this publication may be reproduced, distributed, or transmitted in any form or by any means, or stored in a database or retrieval system, without prior permission of the author.

This is a work of fiction. Names, characters, brands, places, and events are either a product of the author's imagination or used fictitiously. Any similarity to real persons, living or dead, is coincidental and not intended by the author.

Wings of Light Publishing
Gig Harbor, WA, USA

ISBN: 978-1-7357695-6-1

Cover Art and Interior Design by Carrie Butler
Professionally Edited by Chrys Fey

PRAISE FOR BOOK 1

"This is a fast-paced story for teens...Throw in some misunderstandings, space battles, alien races locked in an ancient war, and we have a great escapist mix."

— Elle Cardy, YA Fantasy Author

"I love the diversity of the characters, and not just because some are alien. This series has the potential to become a new-classic, space opera series."

— Toi Thomas, Author

"I enjoyed this lively adventure, a quick read that begins with a movie theater transforming into a spaceship. What a great premise!"

— Carol Riggs, YA Speculative Fiction Author

ABOUT BOOK 2

Amaya is supposed to bring peace to the galaxy.
Which is tough when she's being held for crimes
against the Neutral Zone. Her imprisonment is on
her own ship with her own crew. But close quarters
create tension.

Honestly, her role as Rayatana is a mess.

She may never get to use her powers for anything
good. Not if her teacher continues to keep secrets,
and not if her powers keep harming others. Putting
her mother in a coma should put her in prison, but
she has a mission. She wants to bring peace to her
people. She needs to become the Rayatana.

DEDICATION

To all those readers who find refuge and
adventure in books.

Let's go seek lost worlds and dragons!

"And the Rayatana will be the Nexus for all tuigseach of The Great Galaxy…A nexus of peace or war. All will depend on choice."

The Rayatana Prophecies, Book 1

01

A TRIAL

Amaya peered into the mirror, trying to find her sense of self, her new normal. She wasn't just an Earth girl anymore but a child of three worlds. Still, she looked much the same. Her sienna brown skin, angled cheekbones, and narrow chin were stubbornly hers. Her curly brown hair was up in its usual high ponytail, which she decided was going to have to be enough for the day's events, formal though they might be. She wasn't a talented hairstylist, but that wasn't as important as having control over the dangerous power inside her.

She took a ragged breath, and the glow in her eyes surged.

She exhaled, and the glow ebbed.

After Amaya and her new crew had landed on Cheleth, a planet far from Earth but in The Great Galaxy, for refuge, the Cheleth Council had charged them with war crimes against the Neutral Zone Treaty.

They had thought they could land, find refuge and allies, and resupply. Instead, Chelethian Security Teams had locked down their ship and held them for the crime of committing acts of war in the Neutral Zone and killing a member of an endangered animal species. Representatives from the Cheleth Planetary Council and other Neutral Zone planets would be gathered to determine their guilt or innocence, and the consequences to their actions.

Before Amaya had discovered her tri-world heritage, she'd been caught up in a war between two alien races. On this same spaceship, disguised as an Earth movie theater, she'd crash-landed in the middle of a fight. She'd fought—and killed—to protect herself. The deaths hung heavy on her conscience, but they had been in self-defense. She didn't see how the trial could prove criminal intent, but she was still nervous. Even with a partial memory-cube download, a type of alien tech, Amaya still didn't understand the nuances of the Neutral Zone trial system.

Since they had been locked down to the spaceport and locked up in their ship, Amaya's time had been filled with preparations for the trial, training to get her power under control, and searching for answers about a chip with coordinates on it Chol had pressed into her hands before they'd left Earth. Instead, the chip had filled her with more questions than answers. The ship's crew had been stuck together on the ship for many cycles, but Chol would not talk, not to her, or anyone else, not even to his cousin Sol. And time was running out.

Amaya took another breath. She needed to focus.

Today was day one of the Trial of Integrity, a trial in which they would somehow prove their intentions and the integrity of their characters. Amaya's power reacted to her nerves by roiling inside her. She closed her eyes, bowed her head, and prayed for calm. Despite the various forms of faith she'd encountered on Earth and with the aliens she'd met, she prayed as she'd been taught to as a child. Her faith steadied her, and the power subsided in ripples. She could still feel the core of it, wrapped in her belly and chest, but she had learned to identify the tidal wave inside as the power she contained.

When she opened her eyes, she stepped back from the mirror and glanced down at her clothing. The light gray, short-sleeved shirt had holes with sewn edges on it; one at the naval, two by her collarbones, one in the center of her spine, and two on her shoulder blades. The loose pants, clasped by a cinch at the waist, had holes on the thighs and the back of the shins. The Trial of Integrity clothes had been delivered to their ship by a Chelethian Security Team. The entire back of the shirt had a stylized tree on it, with purple foliage and orange bark and roots that spread down to the hem of the shirt. She fingered one of the carefully stitched holes. The way the seams were so specific made her wonder exactly how and where this Trial of Integrity would take place.

As she started to put on the soft gray boots, someone knocked on her door with a soft rap. It wasn't Sol. Through their shared Zoe Bond, she sensed his drowsy, warm sleep from a nearby room. It was a strange thing to accept in the back of her mind, but it wasn't the only strange thing she'd experienced and accepted as an Earth girl drawn into a war between two powerful alien races. Sol was one of those races. The Zoe Bond between them anchored her, but also worried her. She had kissed him once, and he had been giving her puppy dog eyes ever since. Yes, he was beautiful and exciting, but she had been burned by her first boyfriend, an over-aggressive creep and a liar. She couldn't throw herself at Sol. Wouldn't.

To comfort herself, she traced the design on the front of her necklace's pendant—three interlocking ovals with hard edges like diamonds molded above the surface.

Someone rapped on the door again, harder.

Amaya inhaled, let it out, and then opened the door.

Tanwen, with her white hair and purple cat-like eyes, stood in the narrow, dimly lit hallway with a somber expression. She wore the same outfit as Amaya, but it hung loosely on her frame and accentuated the paleness of her skin and the dark nails on her hands. Tanwen was Ddraigon Kin from the Faerland Arm of The Great Galaxy and Amaya's teacher in the usages of her power. It was strange to see her wearing the same clothes, strange to think she would also be held responsible for the events on Cheleth even though she'd been in a holding cell at the time.

Tanwen cocked her head. "Finally ready for this morning's lesson?"

Tanwen had been training Amaya every morning, both inside the ship and in the forest closest to the North Chelethian Space Port, under close guard by a Chelethian Security Team.

"Do we have time before the trial?"

"There's always time to train, grasshopper."

Amaya rolled her eyes at Tanwen's reference to an old Earth television show about martial arts from the seventies. "You need an updated memory-cube download on Earth culture."

Tanwen chuckled before sobering. "You say that, but you won't accept any more memory-cube downloads for yourself."

Amaya shifted uncomfortably and crossed her arms. The memory-cube download had gifted her with three alien languages and brief information about some of the cultures of The Great Galaxy, and it had done all of that in a tiny amount of time. Yet, it was a piece of convenient alien tech she wasn't comfortable with. "I don't like the sensation I get in my mind when I access new information from the download," she said. "The languages are incredibly helpful, but the rest is dizzying."

Tanwen raised one of her eyebrows. "Exactly. That's why I'll stick with my old Earth knowledge. It helps enough."

Amaya leaned forward. "When are you going to tell me what you were doing on Earth?"

Tanwen's face hardened. She clenched her jaw and spun on her heel. "Your training is more important than stories."

Frustrated by Tanwen's response, Amaya's power flared, but she breathed deeply again before following Tanwen along the short hall of the upper deck and down the stairs into theater two of the spaceship. The movie screen took up most of the wall on one end of the room. The old exit signs were still lit, even though the ceiling lights kept the room bright. In the back of the room, the walls opened up to reveal a small kitchen area. The smell of popcorn continued to fill the air, despite the many meals they had eaten in this room while waiting for the trial.

02

QUESTIONS UNANSWERED

Tanwen sat cross-legged on the hard floor and indicated for Amaya to sit across from her.

Folding her legs under her, Amaya sat and waited.

Tanwen closed her eyes, and as she took deep breaths, her jaw loosened.

Amaya copied Tanwen, who preferred a show-not-tell approach to their lessons.

"Today, I want you to consider a single movement you perform with confidence, something that is as easy as breathing."

Amaya's mind went blank. What skills did she have? She could fight. She had survival skills. She had been trained in martial arts, gymnastics, and dance. Her mom had seen to all that. Mom. The wave of heat in her core hardened, and her breath became rapid.

"Slow your breathing. Think of something good."

Amaya filled her lungs and focused on a memory of her grandparents laughing. The power in her ebbed and flowed into a softer ripple that matched her breathing.

"Now, imagine a single movement, one you enjoy and perform without hesitation."

Amaya pictured her ready stance; one she had learned in fencing and perfected in kickboxing class.

"Now, stand and demonstrate."

Amaya opened her eyes, stood, and got in her stance—feet shoulder-width apart, one foot slightly behind the other so her body was angled toward the center of the space around her, with her hands up but loose, not fists. Ready for offense or defense.

"Good. Now, call your power with confidence."

Amaya's confidence dropped like a stone in her stomach. Her power. She had called it so many times in anger. But the power was there. It wasn't based on her anger. It wasn't based on her fears. Still, it felt unwieldy, as if at any moment she would lose control of the tidal wave and it would overwhelm her and everything around her. "I don't know if that's a good idea."

"You've done it before. You can do it today. Reach into your core, create a shield, and bring it up."

Amaya closed her eyes, found her core, and

pictured a shield layered over her muscles.

"Open your eyes slowly."

Amaya cracked open an eyelid to see she was glowing. Afraid, she gasped. Her power flared before dimming to nothing.

"Try again. Remember, fear is the enemy, trust is the armor, grasshopper."

Amaya grumbled in disagreement. "I will try again, but then, I need an answer to one of my questions." It was a deal they'd made when they first arrived on Cheleth. Tanwen had a way of circumventing Amaya's questions, but she wouldn't get away with it this time.

"If you succeed, then I will answer."

Sighing, Amaya closed her eyes. She imaged the ready stance and drew up her shield, trusting her faith to guide her. She remembered something she had learned from Tanwen earlier. All of her extra strength and speed in a physical combat relied on her unique power, which meant she had been using it unconsciously all along. The power was a part of her. Warmth embraced her, and when she opened her eyes again, her skin was glowing softly.

"Good."

Amaya grinned and let the power ebb back into a solid core inside her. "Now, I get an answer to a question."

"Of course," Tanwen said. "But consider what

you most need to know, today of all days."

Amaya meant to ask Tanwen about her covert operation on Earth, but what came out was the pressing concern under her thoughts, the one haunting her every day. "When will my mom wake up? How can I use my power like this if it hurt her?"

"Your mom is in Med-bay, healing. Meanwhile, you have spent time on grounding techniques, recognizing your power, and creating a shield with it over and over again. I think you can move on to more, but I have been waiting for your mother to wake, so you can have that reassurance. I'm sure she will wake soon."

Right then, Bay entered the room. Her close-cropped dark curls had grown out slightly during their time on Cheleth. Instead of her ever-present Ratterran military uniform with the striking red and brown jacket, she wore the same trial outfit Amaya and Tanwen wore. This didn't stop her from sporting four jewels on her upper lip, which meant she was descended from four generations of high-ranking Ratterran warriors. She often held her chin high, with her lips parted to show the additional ranking tooth jewel she had on her front incisor.

Always abrupt, she barked out, "I don't like the clothes they've given us. These holes are for connection points where they'll attach us to a simulator. We'll be taking the trial inside a machine. I thought the arena would be real, not simulated. This is an insult."

"We'll be inside a machine?" Amaya asked. They hadn't been given any details about the trial, and the others hadn't explained much to her. She poked one of her fingers through the close-stitched hole by her navel and pulled the cloth away from her skin. "Why would this bother you? I thought the Ratterrans preferred technology over power usage."

Bay crossed her arms and scowled. "I don't like my mind being messed with."

Tanwen shook her head. "It is not as you would think. Cheleth's trial simulation will be different because Cheleth, the planet, will be guiding the trial."

Sol entered the theater, wearing the same outfit. "Have you done this before, Tanwen?"

Even when Amaya tried, she couldn't ignore the warmth of connection she had with Sol or the zing of attraction that ran between them. She tried to dampen that feeling. It was all too complicated. She wasn't about to throw herself at him every time he walked into a room, but dang he looked good. His wavy, dark hair, green eyes, olive complexion, and athleticism drew her interest like a moth to a flame. She caught herself checking him out again, glanced away, and noticed Bay's sneer out of the corner of her eye.

What was she going to do about Bay? Bay's continued contempt toward Sol was more evidence of Amaya's failure as the Rayatana. Sure, she had managed to get Bay, her dad Rayal, Sol, Prya, and Geral to answer to her command despite being on opposite sides for a thousand years, but when it came to working together without a direct order, they always found ways not to.

Amaya shook her head. Worrying wasn't helping her get ready for the trial. She held out a hand to Tanwen, who still sat on the floor.

Tanwen ignored it. "I'm not that old." She stood and brushed back her white hair. "We will have to work together in the trial. If there is anything important you need to know, for that immediate task, now is the time."

"What were you all doing on Earth? Why Earth?" Amaya asked.

At the same time, Sol blurted, "What can we expect in the trial?"

Bay threw up her hands. "How can you expect me to work with…?" Bay made a sign with her hand.

Sol growled and stepped toward Bay, his face in a harsh snarl.

Amaya got between them, wishing the memory-cube download had explained some of the slang and insults these two were so familiar with.

They stopped.

Bay huffed out a hard breath and pointed her finger at Sol's chest. "My people were on Earth because the Terrs were there and we needed to know why."

Sol stepped back. "You know why. I've told you. I was there because my aunt, Queen Calanthe of the Terr Protectorate, wanted me out of her way. On the surface, I was in trouble for supposedly charming a young woman I knew."

Bay advanced on him, with her hands in fists.

Sol held up his hands, palms open. "But that's not what happened."

Bay raised her clenched fists and curled inward, as if wrestling with her own anger. She let out a loud breath, that sounded almost like a sob and said, "My mom died while doing the bidding of a Terr charmer. No one should have the ability to force others to do their will with their words."

Shoulders slumped, Sol retreated . "I am so sorry, Bay. I know my people have misused their powers, especially the power to charm. It is wrong. So wrong."

Bay ran her hands down her face, wiping at a glimmer of tears. "I don't know how I can work with Terrs, but my dad expects it. Just like how he expects you"—she paused and gave Amaya a stare—"to unite us."

Amaya didn't know what to say. She pressed her fingers together and brought them to her lips, considering her words. Amaya was responsible for the tenuous truce between the Ratterran ships and the Terr ship. According to the Raya, the quasi-religious group that followed the prophecies involving the Rayatana, she was supposed to create peace and unite The Great Galaxy. It all sounded too grandiose to have anything to do with an Earth girl. Except, she wasn't just from Earth. She was, as the prophecy stated, a Child of Three Worlds. Her maternal grandparents had been Terr and Ratterran. Her mom had raised her to fulfill this crazy prophecy without telling her, and when she had tried to confront her mom about it, Amaya had lost control of her power. The shame of her mom's injuries kept her from checking on her mom in Med-bay, even when she knew she should. It was next on her list of things to do before the trial started. She was expecting people with very real wounds to somehow work together.

After the moment began to feel awkward and Bay stepped back, she held her hands out to the young woman. "We have to work together. What's one thing you need to ask Sol to be able to trust him during the trial?"

"I have nothing to ask him." Bay tilted her chin up and stalked out of the room.

Amaya wrapped her arms around her stomach. "Well, that didn't go well."

Tanwen reached out and put a hand on Amaya's shoulder. "She will come around. Her father trusts you and he trusts her, which is why she's going to the trial as the representative of the Ratterrans."

Amaya sighed. Despite his vow of loyalty, Rayal

had been pacing about the ship in frustration over the Chelethian Security measures. He talked to his people daily, privately, as did Bay. Last night, the Chelethian Security Team had allowed Rayal to visit his old crew. She wondered if he had come back last night. "Rayal has been acting odd, keeping quiet about his conversations with the crews he used to command."

She thought back on the fight she'd had with Rayal back on his ship. It had been bloody, brutal, and fast. She hadn't consciously used her power, but she understood now it must have been what made her fast enough and strong enough to beat him. It was the only way she had won. Rayal had bowed to her as the Rayatana, becoming the first member of her makeshift Honor Guard, and handed off his command to another Ratterran. Both ships had followed them to Cheleth. Both waited for the outcome of the trial.

Amaya traced the duality of symbols on the back of her pendant. The symbol for the Terrs. The symbol of the Ratterrans. They were connected, branches from the same people group, she was sure of it. And yet, Rayal had stopped attempting to connect with the Terr and had started to return to the Ratterrans. She didn't know what she could do, today of all days, to fix things, but she couldn't do much from where she was at. She had an idea, if she could get her eyes on Ratterran ships, she might see something, some clue to what Rayal was up to. "I'm going to the Command Center to see if I can find Rayal. I need to speak to him."."

"Wait." Tanwen strode over to Amaya and gazed at her in concentration. Her brows furrowed. "The Ratterrans will take any question of their honor as an insult."

Amaya shrugged. "I also want to check in with Captain Prya and Pilot Geral, to see if Captain Prya knows when we can expect the Chelethian Security Team to arrive. I'll meet you in the Med-bay to see how my mom is doing."

Tanwen held her gaze steadily and then nodded. "I will see you there."

Sol came over to her and held out his hand.

She took it, squeezed it, let it go. "You and Bay need to make peace." She stepped back. "I'm headed to the Command Center, but could you talk to her?"

Sol ran a hand through his thick, dark hair. "I'll try." He ducked out of the room. A twinge of apprehension came through their Zoe Bond.

That was his emotion. But did she feel guilty, too?

INCOMING

Captain Prya, a tall Terr woman with dark, bushy eyebrows and a proud bearing pointed to part of the hover-screen at her console. "The Ratterran ship stands out because of the sheen of the metal and the boxiness of the design. They take their belief in science over natural systems into their everyday designs, although they do like jewelry, which you've probably noticed. This enjoyment of gem-style decoration comes through on their ship's designations, with the colored dots after each ship name."

Amaya focused on the Ratterran ship. It had a deep blue sheen to the metal surfaces, which did have boxy angles. The name "Lightning" was followed by several silver and red dots.

"Where's the other one?"

Prya gave her a sharp glance. "Didn't Rayal clear it with you?" She smacked the hover-screen closed and stood. "Rayal told me he had your permission. The other Ratterran ship took off late last night to orbit the planet. Chelethian Security cleared them before they left."

"What? Has he returned or did he leave…?" Amaya trailed off.

Prya shook her head. "He wouldn't betray you. You are his commanding officer, as Ratterran custom demands." She poked at something on her console again, bringing the screen back up. "It is one of the things I have always admired about the Ratterran people. They take their honor seriously."

The Ratterran command structure was based on violent contests, according to the little Amaya had learned. It didn't seem like a good measure of leadership to her, although she had taken advantage of it to make Rayal and Bay a part of her crew.

She stared out at the purple and orange forest of Cheleth in one of the large viewing screens and wondered how running for her life in that same forest could seem nostalgic. Weren't normal seventeen-year-olds supposed to yearn for college acceptance letters and prom dates? That life had fallen far behind her.

A sleek black ship roared into the spaceport.

Prya stood and hit her communication button. "A Terr warship has arrived! Everyone to the Command Center."

"I think we should contact the Chelethian

Council before we make any sudden moves." Amaya sat up straight, hoping she looked sure of her decision.

Prya nodded. "Right." She hit another button on her console. "Security? We have an issue. A Terr warship has arrived. It's a small war scout, but don't underestimate them." She paused, waiting for a response.

While listening to the conversation, Amaya watched the screens as the sleek, black ship with three red stars emblazoned on its sides landed near them.

Chelethian Security responded via the communication system, "Stand down. The Terr Scout Bel-25 is here on our invitation, as witnesses for the trial."

Amaya exchanged a startled glance with Prya and waved her hand toward the console. Prya nodded, and Amaya pressed the button. "This is Amaya speaking. May I ask why the Terr War Scout is here as witnesses for our trial?"

"They claim the Terrs with you are traitors to the Terr Protectorate and should not represent their people."

Prya sank into her captain's chair with her shoulders slumped.

Amaya shook her head in disbelief. "Understood, Security. Thank you. We'll continue awaiting our escort."

"Thank you, Rayatana Prime." The voice com clicked off.

Amaya closed the communication system on their end and sat back. "Rayatana Prime?" she repeated.

Prya lifted her chin and sat up straight. "Yes, that's what I logged our ship as when we landed. The Ratterran ships are Rayatana Two and Three until you give them other names. This is acceptable, is it not?"

"Of course," Amaya said. "You chose well."

Prya ran one hand over her command console. "I know my ship is not…the class one might use as a Prime ship."

"It's perfect. I feel at home here." Amaya meant every word, as she considered the command center itself, disguised to look like the ticket booth at a movie theater. She wouldn't have wanted to fly across The Great Galaxy in anything else. As she gazed around the room, she noticed movement on one of the big vidscreens showing the view of the Ratterran ship which was part of her fleet. A figure exited. She leaned in for a better look as Prya did something to her console.

The image clarified. Rayal—his huge frame squeezed into the form-fitting red and brown uniform of the Ratterrans—was walking back to their ship.

Amaya gritted her teeth. He had some explaining to do.

MISSING

Geral, with his dark hair disheveled and his hands half-soapy, entered the command center and immediately wrapped his arms around Prya, as if guessing her mood. Prya, slightly taller than her husband, folded into him, and they held one another.

Amaya turned away to give them privacy and was swept into a one-armed hug from Sol, who stepped into the command center. He gave Amaya a sheepish smile. A wave of hopefulness swept through their Zoe Bond. "I have something for you, something I need to give you before the trial."

Before she could respond, Captain Prya made a chopping motion with her hand. "Bel-25 landed, and they are here to represent the Terr Protectorate in the trial. We have been disavowed."

Sol's jaw dropped, and he stiffened. "Bel-25? That's the ship that landed?" He ran a hand through his hair.

Amaya tightened her arm around him, noticing the waves of anger and grief coursing through him and hoping to offer comfort. "What is it?"

"The captain of the ship hates me. She's probably here to make my life a living hell."

"She'll have to get in line," Rayal said, abruptly entering the room.

Although he was huge compared to her, Amaya stepped away from Sol and planted herself in front of Rayal so he could go no farther in the tiny command center. "Rayal, you and Sol are my allies. Explain yourself. And explain why only one Ratterran ship is currently in the space port." She glared up at the burly Ratterran who had fought her and lost.

Rayal stepped back slightly and flexed his hands. "My daughter is missing."

"How do you even know she's missing when you weren't even here?" Amaya followed Rayal's movements, continuing to close the distance between them.

"I have a neuro-link to her bio-tech. She's currently unconscious, and the link showed she moved to the edge of the ship before it blipped out."

"What? That's...how could that happen?" Amaya pinched her nose, trying to think.

Rayal growled and clenched his hands into fists. "That's what I intend to find out. These Terrs are not honorable people, Rayatana. I know you trust them, but Terr Prince Chol is the scum of the universe. If I find out he has charmed my daughter, I will tear out his throat."

The heat built up in Amaya, threatening to pour out in an uncontrolled way. She closed her eyes before saying, "You will do no such thing, but if he has charmed her, I will deal with him. Now"—she took a deep breath and glared at his feet, noticing with satisfaction that he had stepped back again—"where is the other ship? Tell me."

Rayal squinted. "I thought Tanwen was training you."

Amaya's power flared and ebbed with each breath she took. The room brightened and dimmed accordingly. It was frightening, but she wasn't going to back down.

Rayal held up his hands. "I was worried about the safety of my people. To protect them, and us, I asked them to take one ship up to orbit. They can provide a safe escape if we need one."

Amaya coiled the power back inside of her. "We? As in all of us?"

Rayal glanced at the others, then back at her. "Yes."

Amaya put her fists on her hips. "Next time, clear it with me first."

Rayal huffed out a breath. "You need more training. I can help. But first, we find my daughter."

Amaya's anger was boosted by the anger coursing through Sol. It must have shown in her eyes because Rayal cringed. She closed her eyes. "You may be right," she said. "And we will find your daughter, but you will show me you honor my command by how you treat Sol, Captain Prya, and Pilot Geral. They have not harmed you or dishonored you in any way since you've been on board, correct?"

"Correct, Rayatana. I will do as you command." His conciliatory voice was back, the one she didn't completely trust.

Was Sol's anger messing with her head? She took a step back from Rayal, then turned her attention to Sol, still with her eyes closed. "Sol, I need you to keep your emotions calm, as much as you can. I want you to work with Rayal to search all the quarters upstairs, the projection booth, and storage. I'm going to Med-bay, see if Tanwen saw her there, and visit my mom. Then I'll scour the whole downstairs of the ship."

Sol left the room. Anger and frustration emanated from him, but she tried to brush it away from her thoughts. The farther away he moved, the clearer her thoughts became. The Zoe Bond between them was causing too many problems. She had to find a way to deal with it. Finally, she let out a sigh and opened her eyes.

Rayal stood in front of her, holding up one hand as if to shield himself. "I promise you, Rayatana, I will help you master the problems you are facing. And I will deal with Sol peaceably. He has done no harm to me or my daughter." He glanced at Prya and Geral. "And these Terr have been the most honorable I have ever met. As I said, I will do as you command."

Amaya wasn't sure what he could do to help her, since she had never seen him use any powers, but she nodded. "Thank you."

He gave her a formal salute, pivoted on his heels, and followed Sol out into the corridor.

Amaya traced the three, interlocking ovals on the front of her necklace again. She had to get these people to work together, not just because she had forced them to, but because they could see the benefit of peace.

GUILTY

Entering the Med-bay, Amaya noticed three things: her mom asleep on one of the med-tables, strapped down, her skin pallid under a low-level photo-medicine light; Tanwen sitting near her, with one light-infused hand on her mom's arm; and the open hydroponics unit.

Chol and Bay were not there. Knowing the hydroponics unit led to a secret emergency exit, Amaya feared Chol might've pulled a disappearing act with Bay. She took a step toward the green-glowing unit, but her mom made a soft sound and Amaya turned to her instead.

Waves of guilt swept over her, and Amaya bent inward. Her chest ached from the shame of her own actions. She lifted her hand to her mom's forehead, but let it drop back to her side. It was her fault—her mom's injuries and tenuous hold on life. All of it was her fault. She slumped under the weight of it.

Tanwen's hand stopped glowing with green

light, and she sat back from healing Amaya's mom. "She is mostly healed and will wake any time now. It is only that she has had a shock and the med-table systems are keeping her in a light slumber until she is ready to wake fully.

Amaya hesitated, with her hand wavering at her side, thinking of how she'd almost lost control of her power just moments ago with Rayal. "Are you sure?"

Tanwen placed her hand over Amaya's. "I will show you."

Amaya's heart rate picked up, and the curl of power inside her tightened. "How?"

"Put your hand over mine on her back."

Amaya curled her fingers into her palm. "I could hurt her."

"I'll guide you."

Amaya uncurled her fingers, and Tanwen placed her hand on her mother's back. Warmth wrapped around her fingertips as Tanwen's power flared to life again.

"Do you sense the power?"

"Yes." Amaya wished the power only provided warmth, strength, and speed, not the destructive force it unleashed when she was angry. Every part of her body tensed in fear.

"Take a deep breath, center yourself, and focus

on that power."

Amaya breathed in slowly, held it for a count of three, and then released it, focusing her concentration on Tanwen's hand. The power inside her responded with a trickle of warmth, and she pulled back. "I don't want to hurt her again."

"You won't. I won't let you. Just stay relaxed and focus your thoughts on gentleness and healing."

Amaya focused on allowing the warm core of her power to well up in her and flow outward, but when the power touched her mom, Amaya drew back again. "I can't. I can't hurt anyone again."

Tanwen sighed. "I had hoped you would trust me enough to try. I can block your powers from getting out of control."

"Are you sure?"

Tanwen nodded. "You're strong, but untrained, which means I know how to block you, by siphoning your power."

Amaya blinked. "You can take my power?"

"Or I can send it in a different direction."

Amaya let the idea rest in her mind for a moment while staring down at her mom's beautiful face. She had to believe her mom would heal.

"Where is my daughter?" Rayal shouted as he barged into the Med-bay.

Amaya jumped. She had forgotten all about the reason she was supposed to be there. "She is not here." She waved to the open hydroponics unit. "They could have gone out the escape hatch. We should check."

"Escape hatch?" Rayal's voice was tense, but he wasn't shouting anymore.

Amaya got up to show him. "The one in the hydroponics unit. It's how Sol and I escaped you and your crew when you attacked us."

"Amaya," Sol hissed, coming in behind Rayal.

A twinge of betrayal lit up her chest from the Zoe Bond. Amaya pushed it away from her mind. "He deserves to know where his daughter might have gone, and he is now a member of my alliance, so he can be trusted with the full schematics of this ship."

Captain Prya entered the tiny room, and Rayal shifted.

He took an audible breath, settled his shoulders, and turned to Prya. "Please, Captain, help me find my daughter. I will" — he swallowed — "allow the Rayatana to determine the punishment for your nephew. We believe they left through the escape hatch."

Prya nodded curtly. "One of our sensors was tripped, but I didn't notice it until after you left the command center. I have also scanned the ship's logs. Chol was speaking to Bay in Med-bay just before

Tanwen arrived. Then the logs go dark, but the sensor for the escape hatch was tripped."

"Thank you, Captain." Rayal squeezed his large frame through the hatch and turned out of sight.

Prya followed him.

The waves of Sol's emotions—fear, anxiety, shame, frustration, defensiveness—pushed against Amaya, but she tried to remain calm. "Do you think you should go with them?" she asked him.

Sol shook his head. "No, I don't think Rayal would like that, given how little he trusts Terrs, and I don't want to leave you." He held out his arms.

Tanwen stood abruptly, interrupting their conversation. "Enough of this Love Boat nonsense."

Amaya's head spun. Why was Chol so secretive? What was he doing with Bay? And just how exactly did Chol and Tanwen know each other? The thought of Tanwen being in on Chol's plans did not sit well with her. She held up a hand. "Wait. Both of you. I need to know how you and Chol knew each other before you were imprisoned by Rayal on his ship."

She turned to Sol now. Her power curled, unfurled, and curled again. All this time, why hadn't she been asking him questions? Was it because she was too focused on the Zoe Bond and the tenuous relationship between them? "Your aunt and uncle called Tanwen a traitor. Explain."

Sol squinted slightly in reaction to her powers' glare.

Tanwen grabbed Amaya's hand.

Amaya yanked back, instinctively defending her power, which had started to flow into Tanwen. "Stop."

"When you do." Tanwen's eyes narrowed.

Heat flushed Amaya's skin, but recognizing the danger, she took a slow breath, focused on her mental warrior pose, and drew the power back into her core. "Let go of me and explain."

Tanwen pressed her lips together, stepped back, and slumped into a chair. "I am Ddraigon Kin. The Ddraigon chose the side of the Terrs long ago. As Ddraigon Kin, I have been part of the Neutral Zone and the Raya. I was given specific training as a youngling, and when I failed, I was sent to discover the secrets of the Terrs for the Raya. I was sent to spy on the Terr Protectorate. Chol was my assignment, and it worked well, for I had another assignment of my own and both brought me to Earth."

Sol rolled back on his heels, then forward again. "When we found out she'd been selling secrets to the Raya, she was named a traitor."

Amaya studied Tanwen. "Why Earth?"

Tanwen clasped her hands together in her lap and stared at the ground.

Amaya struggled to maintain her calm. She

wanted answers. She needed to know why her home had been targeted. Was Earth in danger? What were aliens—no, tuigseach from The Great Galaxy doing on Earth in such great numbers?

After what seemed like an interminable wait, Tanwen finally met her gaze. She opened her mouth, but heavy footsteps and grunting from the narrow passage behind the hydroponics unit interrupted her response.

A CHALLENGE

Rayal stepped out of the hydroponics unit, with an unconscious Bay in his arms. He cradled his daughter gently as he carried her to the med-table.

Amaya followed him closely and touched Bay's arm. "What did Chol do?"

Rayal traced Bay's forehead gently with his fingertips. "Captain Prya thinks he charmed her to sleep, no more. The med-table will tell us more."

A synthesized voice spoke, and the table lit up around Bay. "Slowed vital signs. High levels of melatonin. No injuries. The patient will wake if given a small stimulant."

"Please administer," Tanwen said, walking over to stand on the other side of the med-table.

A light flashed over Bay's face, once, twice, three times.

She woke with a start. "No, you…" She glanced

at her surroundings before locking gazes with her dad. "Dad, I tried to stop him, but he told me to go to sleep. I guess I lost him."

Rayal opened his arms. "It's all right. We're going to be okay."

Bay snuggled into him.

Watching the huge Ratterran hold his daughter with tenderness awoke an old yearning in Amaya. Her dad used to hold her like that when she was tiny, but he'd stopped being tender when she'd gotten older.

She turned away.

Sol glanced awkwardly at her, then stepped toward the hydroponics unit. "Aunt Prya?" Sol asked.

"Here," Prya answered, coming out of the hydroponics unit. "He left this behind." She held up a thumb-sized, circular disc with a plastic case. "It's locked, but the way it was placed in the supply bunker, I think he meant for us to find it."

Tanwen held out her hand. "I can open it."

Prya withheld the device, stowing it in her pocket. "We'll examine this together, in the galley with the whole crew." She turned her stern gaze on Amaya. Her face softened.

Amaya sighed. "Let's get the information we can, and then make the decisions we need to move forward." She looked over at Rayal and Bay. "If you can join us, I think we should do this now."

Rayal kept one arm around Bay. "We can join you."

Bay held onto her dad but glared daggers at Sol.

Amaya couldn't change thousands of years of bias in a day, but she wished she could.

MORE QUESTIONS THAN ANSWERS

After Geral brought each of them cups of awak, a stimulating warm beverage that tasted like a cross between coffee and tea, everyone took their seats around the narrow galley table in the common area. Rayal and Bay took one side of the table, while Sol took the other. Tanwen sat at the end of Sol's bench, but not next to him. Amaya sat directly across from Rayal, next to Sol. A gap between her and Tanwen gave Geral plenty of space to sit. Amaya watched to see what Geral would do. Whistling a jaunty tune, he sat down with his cup of awak next to Rayal.

"Do you take yours with any sweeteners?" Geral asked Rayal, pointing to his cup of awak.

"Of course not," Rayal said stiffly, sitting rigid in his chair.

"I'd like some," Bay said quietly, as she leaned on her dad.

"I'll get it," Sol said. He stood to go rummage through one of the cupboards.

Rayal grunted and wrapped an arm around Bay again as if to protect her.

"He's not like Chol," Amaya said. "Plus, you know he's bonded to me."

Rayal tilted his head. "Just how did the Bond come about?"

Amaya shifted her cup of awak in her hands. "He gave me his Word and his Bond. I accepted with the same words I'd heard my grandparents use with each other. I didn't know how serious it was, or that it would be a Zoe Bond, but I felt it when it happened."

Bay tilted her head to the side, considering Sol out of the corner of her eyes. "And how did it feel?"

Amaya shifted slightly in her chair. "Like a jolt of electricity. Since then, if we're angry with each other, it hurts. Other times, I feel a sense of assurance, a connection. And then other times, I can't seem to keep his emotions out of my head."

Bay smirked. "So, he isn't going to make you angry because it will hurt him?"

"Well, we've already made each other angry enough to hurt each other," Amaya said.

"But he has more reason than most Terr to be loyal to you," Rayal said.

"Some of us are Raya," Geral said, "not just Terr."

"Are you?" Rayal asked.

"Yes," Geral said. "Prya and I have been on Earth for a few decades. I was disavowed by my sister, Queen Calanthe, when I decided to marry an exceptional pilot who wasn't a political pawn of the nobility. We found the Raya, or I should say, the Raya found us. My sister outfitted us with this ship disguised as an Earth movie theater and sent us to Earth on a long reconnaissance mission for the Terr Protectorate to find all the Rayatana Candidates." He tapped the table near Amaya. "Your region is one of the main regions we knew to have Rayatana Candidates and also one more forgiving of different faces and features. We lived and worked in your community for twenty years without any incident. When Sol came to live with us, the transition was easy. When we received new orders to search for a missing Terr of high importance, I suspected Chol was involved somehow. Then the Ratterrans came." He paused, glancing at Prya, then back to Amaya. "Before everything happened, when you came to the theater, I knew there was something about you. We suspected you were not fully human. When you accepted Sol's Bond, I thought I saw a flash in your eyes, but I still didn't know you were the Rayatana or even a Rayatana Candidate."

That phrase again. Amaya pressed her fingers

around her cup of awak. "Rayatana Candidates? As in many?"

At the same time, Sol leaned in and said, "Why didn't you tell me you had joined the Raya?"

Geral gave Sol a pointed look. "Would you have joined us?"

Sol fidgeted with his uniform badge. "When I first came, no."

Amaya put her hand on Sol's arm and tapped her cup on the table to gain their attention. "Why would there be Rayatana Candidates on Earth?"

"I can answer that." Amaya's mom limped into the room. She took the seat next to Amaya and wrapped her arms around her.

"Mom!" Amaya threw her arms around her mom. Tears welled in her eyes as she clung to her. "I'm so sorry, Mom. I didn't mean to hurt you. I'm so, so sorry."

Her mom ran her hands over Amaya's curly hair and kissed her on the forehead. "I'm all right."

Amaya didn't know what to think about her mom's easy forgiveness. In the past, she'd given Amaya guilt trips for weeks over the smallest of infractions. Had she changed? Amaya didn't know, but she wanted to pepper her with questions. Instead, she helped her mom into a chair, then sat on the edge of her own, the curl of her tension and power tight inside of her.

"Why do you know about the Rayatana Candidates?"

Her mom bit her lip. "Your grandparents weren't the only ones with a mixed marriage to come to Earth, and they weren't the first. The Raya and many tuigseach have been visiting Earth for at least as long as the Thousand Years' War. It was believed for a long time that the Rayatana might be born on Earth."

Amaya sat still, completely shocked. "So, the whole time I was growing up, you kept all of this from me? That's why you vetted my schools and my friends, why you fought with dad so much, why I had to take all of those classes, and you wouldn't let me lift my head in anger." She glared at the table in front of her, noticing the glow of power reflected off the surface. She took a slow breath, and the glow dimmed, but the power inside her coiled tighter and tighter. "I don't like it when people keep stuff from me."

She shifted her attention to Tanwen. "Speaking of which, I need to know why you and Chol were on Earth. And we need to know what's on that disc he left for us."

Tanwen's shoulders slumped. "I don't know where to start."

"She thought she was the Rayatana." Rayal snorted and rolled his eyes.

Tanwen bowed even more over the table.

"What?" Amaya couldn't believe she'd heard him right.

While they talked, Prya handed the disc to Tanwen. "Tanwen, unlock this and make your explanation quickly, please."

Tanwen pressed her fingertips to the sides of the disc. It glowed briefly, and she handed it back to Prya.

"Your fingerprints unlocked it? Explain. Everything." Amaya clenched her hands into fists on the table.

Tanwen held out her hands to Amaya. "Do you see these?" Her hands glowed, and then her fingers elongated and shifted into claws with dark talons at the tips. After a moment, shifted them back to their human-like appearance. "I am part Glower, part Ddraigon, and part Elvesan."

Amaya loosened her fingers. "That means you're a child of three worlds, like me. So, why aren't you the Rayatana?"

Tanwen continued to stare at the table. When she spoke, it came out woodenly. "It is not so simple."

Amaya's mom lifted her chin. "She is not Terr, Ratterran, and a third world. The Terr and the Ratterran tuigseach have made war for a thousand years. The Rayatana must come from a child who shares the heritage of the Terrs and the Ratterrans."

Tanwen narrowed her eyes at Amaya's mom.

"Exactly. My parents and my people did not understand that, though. They raised me to be what you are, but I did not pass the tests. When that happened, I disappointed everyone. I didn't know what to do, so I went in search of the true Rayatana, hoping to fulfill my training."

Sol brushed his hand against Amaya's arm. "And you went to Earth?"

Tanwen sat up straighter. "Not at first. First, I found histories, legends, stories, and the Raya. When I was watching Chol and reporting back to the Raya, I discovered Chol was on his own search for Rayatana Candidates."

Amaya's breath hitched. "Candidates? You keep saying that. There are many?" Maybe she wasn't the only one. Maybe she didn't have to fulfill the role everyone expected her to fill.

Sol raised his hand. "How is that possible? I was told Chol ran off on some holiday and disappeared."

Tanwen slouched again. "He was commissioned by your queen to find the Rayatana Candidates and bring them to the Terr Protectorate. He did. And they disappeared."

Shocked into stillness, Amaya forced herself to breathe. Surprise and anger coursed through the Zoe Bond from Sol as he struggled with this new information, too. He hadn't known. Amaya centered herself, staring into her cup of awak. "How many Rayatana Candidates are there? And if there are many, how can I be the Rayatana?"

Tanwen pressed her lips together and stood. "I know you are the Rayatana." She held up her hand and counted on her fingers. "The vision I had. The choice you made to free me. Your heritage. You have a bond with a Terr. Terrs and Ratterrans follow you. The coordinates Chol left you. Now, this." She pointed to the disk Prya held. "These are all the reasons I know you are the Rayatana we've been waiting for."

Amaya swallowed back a protest. "What do the rest of you think?" She gazed at each of them for a few seconds at a time, measuring their initial reaction.

Rayal met her eye and nodded. Next to him, Bay cocked her head and made a slight nod with a shrug. She wasn't as sure.

Geral put his hand to his heart. "As Tanwen said, you are the Rayatana. The coordinates from the first disk, despite the lack of information from Chol, pointed us to the heart of the conflict at Ganyth. Only the Rayatana will be able to solve that."

Prya put her hand on her husband's shoulder and bowed her head in Amaya's direction. "This is true."

"We all know," her mom said. She tapped her fingers on the table as she often did when she was about to launch into something she knew Amaya wouldn't like. "I would have told you, but your father didn't believe me, and I didn't know how. Then my parents died, the divorce happened, and we moved. This is all happening so quickly. I didn't expect you to leave on that ship." She leaned against Amaya. "I will help you. I know what leadership skills you need."

Amaya shifted away from her mom, feeling a bit of the old anger burning in her again. She dropped her gaze to the table, in case her power surged. "I need training."

"And we will train you," Tanwen said. "All of us."

Amaya took a long gulp of her awak. The dark bitter liquid eased down her throat. She imagined she felt the caffeine from it energizing her for everything she needed to do.

"Please, tell us more about the Rayatana Candidates," Amaya said.

LOYALTIES

Tanwen began to pace back and forth. Finally, she turned to face them and said, "There have been many children of three worlds, some even who have the heritage of five or more worlds, but none with Terr and Ratterran heritage. As you may have guessed, The Great Galaxy has patterns of life, a sense of unity in its diversity. For those who believe in the Triple One, these patterns fit within our faith. For those who believe in Xia, it fits their faith. For those who believe in chaos and chance, it is harder, but they make reasons for it to be so. Your own Earth has many of these beliefs, renamed in different ways, and more beliefs than those I know. You will have to make peace with the patterned heritage of The Great Galaxy in your faith.

"But I digress. Earth is home to many Rayatana Candidates because of several excursions and two noteworthy landings of tuigseach from various parts of The Great Galaxy. These tuigseach discovered they were, or could be, compatible with life on Earth, as bystanders and as parents. They, and their children, have been called demons, angels, witches, gods, heroes, villains, superheroes, or fantastical beings. The current name for them is Anomalies. I have met many of them. They all have abilities, which we often call powers or gifts.

"There are groups of Anomalies who band together on Earth. There is a group that hunts them down and forces them to register with a secret international organization. But they did not find you or know of you. I know this because we used their database to find many others. At first, I helped Chol. Then we became at odds when the Rayatana Candidates began to disappear. I don't know what happened to them."

She wrung her hands. "I was responsible for those children. I have to help them, if they can be helped, and to do that, I have pledged myself to your service, Amaya. As the Rayatana, I believe you will bring peace to The Great Galaxy and make it possible for all tuigseach to live freely."

Amaya leaned forward. "We need to review that disk from Chol, but I hate to trust information from someone who traffics in children."

Tanwen held up a hand. "Before Rayal and his crew captured us for crimes against the Neutral Zone on Earth, Chol found out I was spying on the Terr Protectorate. He admitted to me then that he stopped turning the Rayatana Candidates over to his superiors in the Terr Intelligence Force. I believe he did not know what the Terr were doing to them until two were lost."

"Lost?" Amaya asked.

Tanwen crumpled in on herself. "Killed."

"You are sure?" Prya asked.

"I saw one of their bodies. I believe the other suffered the same fate."

"But where are the ones Chol didn't turn over to his superiors?"

"He wouldn't tell me. We had lost trust with each other by then."

Prya stood. "I am ashamed. Our people are shamed by this." She ripped the Terr badge off her uniform. "I will no longer be called Terr."

Geral tore off his badge, too. "And I am no longer a son of the Terr Royal Line." He threw his badge on the table.

Sol reached up for his badge, but he hesitated.

His shame and doubt came through their Bond.

"Don't," Rayal said and held out his hand to Sol. "We must keep the appearance of at least one loyal Terr. And"—he shifted his gaze to Bay, and then to Amaya—"if we are to truly broker peace, we cannot all be Ratterrans."

Sol dropped his chin. "You are an honorable tuigseach. Pride of your people."

Amaya put her hand on his arm.

"A Terr royal apologizing to me? That is another sign that we are with the Rayatana." Rayal grinned at Amaya, and then he held out his hand to Sol. "If we keep our loyalty to the Rayatana, then we are brothers."

Sol took Rayal's hand in his, not in a traditional Earth handshake but in an arm-wrestling match position. They squeezed each other's hands a moment before letting go.

Rayal offered his hand to Geral, and then to Prya. They also pledged their loyalty to Amaya and their alliance.

A warm bubble of hope spread from Amaya's core, growing outward. Without knowing how it was happening, her skin glowed and her eyes became beams of light. She snapped her eyelids shut.

"It is not the same," Tanwen said. "You can open your eyes. I will show you."

Amaya swiveled her head toward Tanwen's voice and cracked her eyelids open. The beams of light coming from them were a warm yellow, not a bright bluish-white. Nothing was hurt in their path. Tanwen radiated the same yellowish light from her skin.

Amaya gaped. "How?"

"The power takes many forms. It is linked to your emotions, so you must exercise self-control."

Amaya shook her head. "I can't always shove

my emotions down."

"No, we don't force our emotions back inside, but we choose how we act on them. It is not the same. It is release, with self-control." Tanwen's skin stopped glowing. "I have learned to use my anger as a catalyst for the healing side of my power. You can do the same."

Amaya nodded. When she relaxed, her body dimmed, and the light beams from her eyes disappeared.

Her mom crossed her arms. "Are you sure you can teach her that level of control? Amaya has never demonstrated an ability to control her emotions. She's always had a temper and the willfulness of something wild." She faced Amaya. "I don't think you should use your power. It's too dangerous."

"She must train or it will ruin her life." Tanwen walked over and put her hand on Amaya's shoulder. "I vow to you, Amaya Iris Benson, that you will have all the training I can give you."

Amaya's chest felt lighter. "Thank you."

Amaya's mom looked to Rayal for help. "Surely, you can't agree with her?"

Rayal held up one of his fingers and the tip glowed with a faint power. "The Ratterrans do not believe in using the gifts to get our way, to manipulate others, or to make our lives easier, but we do believe in learning control."

Sol gasped. "I thought the Ratterrans didn't

have powers."

"We choose to use them as a last resort," Bay said, speaking up for the first time. "We don't flaunt them all over and bully the rest of The Great Galaxy with them."

"Not all Ratterrans have powers, and not all Terrs have powers." Geral shrugged. He fixed his gaze on Amaya's mom. "What did your parents share with you about powers?"

She glared at Geral and curled her lip in disgust. "My father told me he never used his powers. Ever."

Rayal ticked his fingers, creating a list of arguments in the air. "But he had them, which meant he could exercise self-control, which takes training."

She threw her hands up and leaned back in her chair. "You don't understand. Consider what Amaya did to me. She is dangerous."

A hollow pain of guilt wormed into Amaya, and she curled her shoulders inward, flashing back to her last moments on Earth, when all the secrets kept and the lies told by her mom had hit her and she'd exploded with power, knocking her mom to the ground when she'd turned her gaze on her. She'd almost killed her mom. What if she'd had? What if she hurt someone else she loved? Her power was overwhelming, too much. She didn't want it.

"Stop." Tanwen squeezed Amaya's shoulder.

"Do not flog yourself with guilt." She glared at Amaya's mom. "Your daughter has already apologized. Forgiveness is needed."

Her mom splayed a hand over her chest. "I forgive her, but I don't think she should…"

Prya interrupted her with a chopping hand motion. "I think you need more time to rest and consider your words. I will walk you back to the Med-bay."

Her mom put her hand on Amaya's arm and gripped it hard. "Feel that muscle. I helped you build that. I trained you and sent you to the best teachers I could afford. I kept you hidden from anyone who might come after you. You know I know what's best."

"No, I don't." Amaya wrenched her arm out of her mom's tight grip. The power building in her responded to her temper, and she closed her eyes, took a breath.

"Center yourself in something positive," Tanwen instructed. "Pray, to whomever you pray to, think of joy."

Amaya pictured a moment at her grandparent's farm, standing in the sunshine and laughing at bubbles floating into the sky. Her anger diminished, and the pull of the power inside her let go. She took a deep breath and placed her hand on her pendant, fingering the grooves of the three symbols on it. Everything came back to who she had to be, who she was meant to be. She leaned toward her mom. "Tell me why we moved away from my grandparents to live in California."

Her mom crossed her arms over her chest. "They were…they had their ideas about you. They were wrong."

Amaya stood, unable to sit any longer and listen to her mom's excuses. "What if they were right? What did they think?"

Her mom stared down at the table in front of her. "That doesn't matter now."

Amaya shook her head. "It does matter. I love you, Mom. I'm sorry I hurt you, but I am not going to follow your grand plan." She had tried to keep the joyful memory in her mind, but her frustration warred with her self-control. Anger burned inside her, and the heat grew. She wasn't sure if her mom would ever trust her again. She didn't even know if she trusted her mom, but she had to move forward. She had to figure this whole mess out.

Tanwen lifted one hand to her mom's head, and her mom slumped over, unconscious.

Amaya jumped up. "What did you do to her?"

Tanwen held out her hands. "Please, Amaya, she was hurting you with her words."

Sol laid a hand on his chest. "I could feel it, and she needed to be stopped."

Amaya clenched her teeth, and then she forced herself to relax her jaw. "My mom is my problem. Not yours. Next time the conversation gets tough, let me handle it."

Sol dropped his eyes to the ground.

Tanwen reached out and touched her mom's head.

She jerked awake and moved away from Tanwen. "You put me to sleep!"

Tanwen crossed her arms. "I did what I did to protect your daughter from you."

Her mom leaned toward Tanwen, jaw clenched. She spoke through her teeth. "Don't you dare do that to me again."

Tanwen lifted her chin. "I'll do whatever I need to do to protect your daughter."

Amaya clenched her fists. Her power responded, and her hands flared with power. She closed her eyes and took a deep breath. "No. You. Won't. Either of you." She took another deep breath and the power inside her coiled into a tight spring. "I will become the Rayatana based on my own choices. You will both fall under my command, regardless of our relationship or your experience."

Her mom stood, gripping the tabletop. "I am your mother."

Amaya covered one of her mom's hands with her own. She allowed a tiny trickle of power into the palm of her hand. It warmed her mom's skin. "I need to train, Mom. This power I have inside me is something I have to control, which means I cannot be following the orders of someone who does not understand it or accept it."

READY OR NOT

A harsh beeping sound filled the galley.

Captain Prya hit a button on her wrist-com, and the beeping stopped. "We have an incoming message from Chelethian Security. I'll play it through the ship's internal speakers."

Amaya gazed contemplatively at the wall-screen, waiting.

Prya touched another button on her wrist-com. "This is Rayatana Prime, Captain Prya speaking."

A clear, baritone voice filled the room. "This is Vidarr Nasenth, Team Leader of Chelethian Security Team One. We'll be your representatives' escort to the trial. Only the trial representatives may leave your ship until the trial's conclusion. We made an exception for Rayal, but we will not make one again. Is this clear?"

Prya answered Chelethian Security. "Yes, we understand and comply."

"Please send out your representatives in a quarter standard."

"We will." Prya turned off the communicator and faced the group. "We need the information on Chol's disc now. We have declared our loyalties, and we understand Amaya's need for training. Now we need to focus." She put the disc into a port, clicked a button on the wall, and a holographic vid-screen lit up the center of the room.

On the vid-screen, text appeared. Use this data with care. Signed Chol Windras Terr, Prince of the Terr Royal Family, and loyal member of the Terr Protectorate.

"Even when he can't speak, he brings the drama." Amaya murmured.

Bay snorted. "Terr."

Sol tensed, and Amaya felt it through their Zoe Bond, but he remained silent as the vid-screen text continued, along with a voice recording from Chol. Unlike his normal schmoozing charm, Chol's voice was quiet.

"In accordance with Protectorate Directive Five-One-Five, I was tasked with finding all the Rayatana Candidates on Earth. After finding them, I was ordered to bring each candidate to a holding station, where Terr and the Noman Group combined their efforts to keep any alien activities on Earth a secret."

"That's not right," Geral said. "The Nomans are…"

The recording continued. "The Nomans were zealous, not because they believe as we do, that the Rayatana must be controlled by the Terr, but because they are attempting to take control of all Anomalies, as all human-alien offspring are called on Earth."

Chills ran down Amaya's arms. The Terr thought they could control her? Or anyone like her? How could she not know about an organization out to control her and people like her? She glanced at her mom and fully realized, even if she was misguided, her mom had protected her.

"After two initial drop-offs of Rayatana Candidates to the holding station, I decided that to continue to work with the Nomans was not in the best interests of the Terr Protectorate. They…harmed the children."

The recording continued, but now the rotating hologram above the table began to take shape. "I have made a new contact with an entity I thought extinct. The entity created a safe space for the Rayatana Candidates and any other tuigseach who need safety on this planet."

The holographic display showed a star system now. It expanded to show The Great Galaxy, zeroed in on one arm of the galaxy, and then deeper into the star system. A glowing green planet surrounded by several rings of asteroids hung like a jewel in dark space.

"That's not Ganyth," Geral said.

"It's the Glower's twin world, the one they don't allow anyone to visit," Sol said.

"A neutral planet," Bay added.

The recording continued. "The entity I contacted told me that some of the Rayatana Candidates and other tuigseach have been sent to work in a prison encampment on Ganyth, within the Terr Protectorate. Its evidence was irrefutable."

The holographic display shifted to show the star system in which Ganyth was located, then the planet itself. "I urge you to go to Ganyth and free those imprisoned, but do not do so without preparations, and do not trust everyone you meet."

The holographic display winked out, and the vid-screen went dark.

But the recording continued. "I am a loyal Terr, and I believe our people have been led astray by those in power, namely my mother, Queen Calanthe. It is not the way of the Terr to exploit others."

Bay gave a sarcastic laugh. "It isn't?"

"This message will self-destruct. I advise you to dispose of it immediately."

Prya pulled out the disc and threw it into a metal bin with orange markings on the container. After she'd closed the lid and locked it, a loud bang went off inside the bin.

Amaya sighed and directed her attention to Tanwen. "Why would he leave if he was going to tell us all of that anyway?"

"It's a test," Tanwen said.

Amaya shook her head. It was the last thing she needed right now. Another test.

Tanwen ran a hand through the side of her hair. "He has seen many Rayatana Candidates fail the basics of what it means to be the Rayatana, including me. So, this is his test for you."

Bay stood. "It's a trap."

"Of course, it's a trap." Sol scowled.

"He did say we should prepare ourselves," Geral said.

Bay shrugged and leaned against table. "He didn't say 'we' should do anything. This is her test." She cocked her head at Amaya.

Amaya opened her mouth to give a quick answer, and then she lowered her gaze to the tabletop. "Trial first, test later. We need to leave."

Sol pointed his finger at Bay. "You aren't the judge of Amaya."

Bay lifted her chin at him. "Who says I'm not? A Terr who tricked her into a Bond to save his people?"

Amaya held up her hand. "Stop." She glanced at Bay, then Sol. "You're both going to judge me, along with everyone else in The Great Galaxy. It's part of the problem. As I said, we need to leave now." Pivoting on her heel, she strode out of the room. They could follow her or get out of her way.

Sol caught up with her in the entryway of the theater-spaceship and put his hand on her arm. She put her hand on his in return, gave it it a light squeeze, and then strode out of the ship and into the spaceport.

The sun shone brightly overhead. Dressed in tan uniforms with the Chelethian symbol of the great tree, the Chelethian Security Forces were varied species of tuigseach. Amaya gazed at them. Elvesans, Ddraigons, two Glowers, several Dryadarians, some beings she didn't know and couldn't classify, a humanoid with wings, and another with a tattoo pattern trailing down her cheek who stood as tall as Amaya's waist but carried two axes strapped to her back, a bandolier of throwing knives, and two grenjen holstered to thigh-high boots. The others had weapons, but this one appeared extra-prepared.

One of the Dryadarians, who had familiar features, spoke for the group. "Crew of the Rayatana, you will put down your weapons and come with us to stand trial on behalf of your tuigseach alliance."

Amaya didn't have any weapons, so she spoke to her group, "You heard him. Please put down your weapons."

"We are unarmed, Rayatana, as we knew we would be entering a peaceful court," Tanwen said.

Sol nodded when Amaya glanced at him.

But Bay withdrew a knife from under her sleeve and held it out, palm up to the Dryadarian. "It's my favorite."

He sheathed the knife in one of his belt compartments. "I will keep it safe for you."

The Terr Scout Bel-25, sleek and bearing the symbol of the Terrs, opened its hatchway.

"Trouble," Bay hissed.

"Don't forget who you're with." Amaya took a few steps in front of her group, glanced back at them, and then over at the Chelethian Security Team. None of them looked overly concerned, but she was. The Terr prided themselves on their use of powers. Tanwen's power had depth and precision from training, but Sol didn't have as much, Rayal had lit up his finger once, and Bay's powers were unknown. Amaya didn't have control over hers, and she wasn't sure how the Chelethians planned to contain them all.

Five figures stepped out of the Terr ship and into the sun. Their black uniforms clung to their athletic figures.

Sol let out an audible groan. "It's her."

The athletic young woman with light brown skin and dark hair pressed into a gleaming bun appeared nothing like Amaya had pictured. Normally, she'd always believed a women who said they were hurt by a man, but this woman radiated cruelty in the set of her jaw and her curled upper lip.

Amaya glanced over at Sol. "We're going to be all right." She said this, despite feeling a wave of anxiety coming through their Zoe Bond.

He swallowed, and she took a step toward him.

The woman sneered and addressed Sol, without even glancing at the others. "I should have known you would betray the Terr Royal Protectorate." She glanced scornfully at Amaya. "I see you've shown what you like in women—disgusting Earther scum of the universe."

Amaya's lips twitched, and then, she forced a laugh, which bubbled up into real laughter because of her nervousness. Everyone turned toward her, with their mouths open in shock.

The woman stepped back and glared at her. "What is so funny?

"You're obviously jealous," Amaya said. As a child, she had discovered as a child that bullies hated to be laughed at. The woman started their conversation with an insult, so Amaya responded. It hadn't been her best response, but...it had turned the tide on the conversation.

"I'm not…I would never be…He's a traitor to Terr." She grabbed her grenjen, a photonic weapon she had in her utility belt, and aimed it at Sol.

Amaya stepped in front of him.

Then Tanwen jumped between them. "Enough."

"Yes, enough." The spokesperson of the Chelethian Security Team raised his hands.

The woman sheathed her grenjen, glanced down as if repentant, and then she raised her head and glared at Tanwen. Her eyes glowed like twin suns.

Sol shrank back, squinting, but Amaya stood her ground. She didn't feel angry, didn't feel the heat of her power inside of her, but she stared into the woman's glare and didn't flinch.

Tanwen did the same.

The woman's eyes flickered. Their intensity lessened. "What are you?" she asked Amaya.

"I am the Rayatana."

"Yeah, right. I've killed a few of those."

A spark of rage burned inside of Amaya. "You've killed children from Earth?"

The woman sneered again. "They were pitiful."

Amaya's eyes lit up the entire hangar. The rest of the Terrs winced.

The Chelethian Security Team closed around them, and their leader pressed a button on a device at his waist.

A throbbing pounded Amaya's skull. "What is…what did you do to me?"

The woman winced, too. "You have power dampeners. I thought those didn't…weren't finished yet."

"The prototypes have some issues, like pain." The Dryadarian grimaced when he noticed Amaya massaging her temple. "I apologize for the inconvenience, Rayatana. I wish I had known who you were when we first met."

Understanding filled Amaya. "You were our driver the last time we were here?"

He gave her a small smile. "Yes. I am not flowering at the moment, or you would see my distinctive patterns."

The Terr woman crossed her arms. "How is this a fair trial if you know her?"

The Dryadarian flicked a glance at her before peering around at the others. "I turned in the Rayatana, the Terrs, and the Ratterrans for the incident of violence that took place on Cheleth, even though this one" — he tilted his head toward Sol — "attempted to buy my silence." He gestured at the Terr woman. "And I am not going to determine her fate. I am merely the head of this Security Team unit. If I behave unfairly, my second will relieve me of command, and she will have my blessing." He glanced at the woman carrying the most weapons. "Narra, what say you?"

Narra raised her tattooed eyebrow. "I haven't seen any problems yet, but when I do"—she patted her grenjen—"it's set to stun for friends like you, Vidarr."

Vidarr held out his hands. "See, we are fair." He gave a slight nod to the Terr woman. "Now, Belryus and Bel-25 crew, drop your weapons. You will not need them in a peaceable trial."

Belryus snorted derisively but dropped her grenjen and some other weapons from her utility belt. Her crew did the same.

When they had finished, Vidarr scrutinized his team. "Form up."

The Security Team surrounded them but shaped themselves into an oval. Vidarr took the front of the oval and pointed to either side of him. "Amaya and Belryus, you will walk with me."

Amaya went to take her place on his right.

Belryus took her place next to Amaya, sneering the whole time.

Amaya wondered if her face was stuck that way. She focused her gaze ahead, noticing the strength of the Zoe Bond as Sol's emotions about Belryus hit her in waves—anger, hurt, fear. With her power blocked and the throb of the dampener in her head, she had thought she wouldn't be able to sense Sol, but she still did. The

Zoe Bond was more powerful than she had thought, or just different; she wasn't sure.

As Vidarr led Amaya, Belryus, and their teams through the spaceport, Amaya realized the hangar was deserted of all the crews and tuigseach she had seen the last time she'd been on Cheleth a few days ago. Was everyone awaiting the trial? Was she considered that dangerous?

THE WALK

As they walked through the port shopping district, Amaya felt like they were being watched, and the feeling was coming through her Zoe Bond. Sol had a rough upbringing—he tested every meal he ate for poison—but she hadn't realized he would be so edgy. It was getting to her again, and she wondered what she could do to put a dampener on it. There had to be a way.

A blinding flash of light followed by an exploding canister of smoke sent Amaya to a kneeling position. She covered her face with her hands.

Sol crouched by her, touching her shoulder as she blinked through her fingers. Her eyes teared up from the acrid smoke.

"Try not to breathe it in." Vidarr handed her a fold-able cloth breathing mask he'd taken out of one of the many pockets on his uniform.

She took the mask and held it over her face,

while he strapped his own on behind his head. Then he reached over and clasped hers securely, before putting on a pair of goggles. He fished around in his gear and pulled out another pair for her.

Amaya took them and slipped them on. Her eyes still stung, but she could see.

A group of Terrs, dressed like Belryus, came through the smoke, wearing gas masks and goggles.

Around Amaya, the others in their party were either struggling to breathe or putting on masks of their own.

Vidarr put on muffs over his ears and motioned to Amaya to cover her own. A second later, he drew two things from his belt—a tiny horn and a grenjen. He flipped a button on the horn, and a blast of sound ripped through the air.

Amaya put her fingers in her ears, but the sound still screamed into her skull, which already throbbed from the power dampener.

When she squinted around her, she saw everyone crouched and blocking their ears, many of them curled on the ground. Only the Chelethian Security Team had ear muffs.

The Chelethians apprehended a dozen Terr soldiers while Vidarr continued to overwhelm everyone with sound. When the Terrs within the nearest area had been cuffed and disarmed, Vidarr stopped hitting the horn.

Amaya withdrew her hands cautiously from her ears. They rang with the echo of the sound, high-pitched and keening. Her head pounded.

Next to her, Sol stood, while rubbing his hands over his ears.

Amaya glanced around and noticed someone from their ship was missing. "Bay?"

"She ran into the shop, over there," Tanwen said, pointing to a shop of loose garments and scarves. She glanced at Vidarr. "I can get her."

Vidarr nodded. "Narra will accompany you."

Narra stalked toward the shop.

Amaya took a step in that direction, but Vidarr stopped her with an outstretched arm. "No, you'll stay here. It's safer."

"For who?" Amaya asked.

"Everyone."

Sol offered her his hand. She took it and stared at the shop door in anticipation.

The door opened, and a Glower came toward them. The Glower, like all Glowers Amaya had seen, was taller than any human, bald with large dark eyes and two flowing, fin-like appendages trailing down their back from their shoulder blades.

The Glower surveyed the group, unblinking,

before focusing on Vidarr. "Team Leader Vidarr. The Ratterran is safe with me."

Vidarr held up his hands and raised his eyebrows. "You know there is a trial, Citra. She needs to come with me."

Citra nodded her head to him. "I will bring her. Tanwen as well."

Vidarr put his hands on his hips. "You know those weren't my orders. Birk Glowfire won't be pleased. He is the Branch of Cheleth because you refused the honor."

The fins on Citra's back wafted forward, glowing a faint purple. "The honor rests upon me still and I have the right to accept, even after so much time has passed. Cheleth knows me. The Trial of Integrity is for Birk's benefit. I will speak to the Ratterran and to Tanwen to assess the Ratterran's part in this."

Vidarr sighed. "You'll testify to this?"

"Yes." Citra gave Amaya an appraising look. "It is good you are here, Rayatana. I am Citra Gia, mother of Lumien, once of the Glower Margos. We will speak again."

Citra sought out the gazes of the other Glowers on the Chelethian Security Team and gave them each a small nod, which they returned with bows. After this, she walked back into her shop.

Narra strode out, scowling. "Vidarr, what is the

meaning of this?"

Vidarr ran one of his hands over his leafy head. "Citra is…Citra. She will take care of them. She will testify."

Narra growled. "Citra. She thinks she knows everything, like many of her kind." She gave a sharp glance to one of the Glowers on the Chelethian Security Team. The Glower raised one bony eye-ridge and shrugged.

"Knock it off, both of you. We all know Glowers have…abilities and knowledge they cannot give us." He surveyed the whole group, resting his eyes on the Terrs who were cuffed in the center of the group. "Let's move."

The Chelethian Security Team surrounded their prisoners in a tighter knot, so much so that Amaya was pressed between Sol and Belryus.

Belryus hissed when they brushed shoulders, but she didn't say anything.

Amaya didn't like being shoulder to shoulder with Belryus anymore than the Terr liked being shoulder to shoulder with her.

Belryus elbowed Amaya in the side once, but Amaya didn't react immediately. The next time that sharp elbow came in her direction, Amaya blocked it with her hand and poked her fingers into the sensitive pressure points at Belryus's elbow joint. Belryus winced away from her and jostled the Chelethian Security member on her other side, an Elvesan with sharp pine-like quills sticking out of their bare arms and face.

Finally, Belryus fell into step with Amaya and stopped pestering her.

The rest of the walk to the trial was uneventful and eerily quiet. The Chelethian Security Team had shown their training expertise, and their ability to block power. This gave Amaya time to think. Review and reassess. Even though she was frustrated by her mom's attitude, her mom's training had helped her so far. The idea of reviewing and reassessing wasn't a bad one, so she took stock of the situation.

She and her closest allies, as well as representatives from the Terr Protectorate, were being charged with crimes against the Neutral Zone, by breaking the neutrality. Not long ago, she'd defended herself in a photonic firefight with grenjens in a nearby forest area, shot two Ratterrans in self-defense, and shot a Nardel, a native predator to Cheleth, who had attacked them while protecting its nest. That same day, she had a trial by combat with Rayal and had taken him and his two crews of Ratterran ships into her alliance, despite the deaths of three members of his crew. She had avoided talking to him about that, which made it worse.

She had excused herself from making amends with her urgency to get home and all that had happened.

If she hadn't rushed home unprepared, if she hadn't misused her power on her mom, if she hadn't run from Earth's Space Defense Force, things would be different. She should have taken more time to plan and taken the time to make amends with Rayal and the Ratterran crews. If she was the fabled Rayatana, then that meant she was responsible.

But what did it mean to be the Rayatana?

It didn't just mean the Child of Three Worlds. Tanwen fit that description. Many others did as well, such as the Rayatana Candidates Chol and Tanwen had tracked down on Earth. The Terrs were responsible for capturing, and possibly killing, Earth-born Rayatana Candidates, all of whom may have had the same right to be called the Rayatana as Amaya did. She wasn't as special as everyone seemed to think.

Why did Tanwen have that vision about her? It had been real. She was sure of that. Tanwen didn't normally get all deep-voiced and weird. Well, she was not normal by human standards, definitely alien, but her usual demeanor didn't include voicing prophecies at every turn. So, Amaya was back to square one. She was supposed to be the Rayatana, even though others might qualify. Did she have a choice?

Tanwen had said something about choices during that vision. Three paths, three choices, three destinies: love, or peace, or death.

Why did her three destinies have to be so

dramatic? And why was it love or peace? Those two should go together. Love and peace.

If her first choice to free Tanwen from imprisonment had been linked to those destinies, it seemed as though she was headed toward peace. But what did the Zoe Bond mean?

And was she really the Rayatana if she ended up dead? She didn't want to end up dead. The thought of it opened a hollow spot in her rib cage.

She put that thought aside.

Was this trial going to be one of her choices? Had hurting her mom accidentally in anger been one of her choices? Leaving Earth and her dad behind? She didn't know. She wanted, no, needed, more information. Maybe she would get it at the trial. She didn't want to be imprisoned on Cheleth, but she did deserve the consequences for her actions. Even in self-defense, she hadn't liked killing those Ratterrans. Would Rayal think she was weak if she told him that? The Ratterran culture fought for leadership in trials and battles. Or would he appreciate her condolences? She didn't know. She tried to tap into the memory-cube as she walked, but she'd been blocking it, so the information didn't come to her.

The Terr-based memory-cube didn't have much information on their sworn enemies, which was something Amaya had found lacking. Rayal had offered her a Ratterran memory-cube, but she hadn't used it after discovering from Tanwen that too many downloads could have adverse effects.

Review. Reassess.

She didn't have time to reflect properly. After a tense and quiet walk through the marketplace of the spaceport and through an area of larger structures, they walked up a set of stone steps into a pillared building. It was similar to Greco-roman in design, except the pillars were made of living trees and the roof was a canopy of leaves and branches. The stones had been built around the roots, or so it seemed, as the roots formed a structure around the stairway.

At the top of the stairs, Amaya glanced back over her shoulder at Sol. They were linked, but it was good to see the determination in the set of his jaw. They were in this together.

THE ARENA

As the group walked into the leafy atrium, Amaya noticed the way the Chelethian Security Team relaxed around her. They were in their home territory. Tuigseach of all different planets lined the walls of the building.

Vidarr led the group into a space beyond the leafy atrium. This space turned out to be a spiral staircase leading down. It was wide enough for three to four people across, but Amaya hunched her shoulders and glanced back up the stairs. She didn't like going underground. Folding her arms around her stomach, she followed Narra and the rest of the group down the stairway, jostling elbows with Sol until he reached out and offered his hand. She intertwined her fingers with his, and a zing came through the Zoe Bond.

At the bottom, the staircase opened up into a cavernous room with stone and dirt walls held in place by giant roots, presumably from the trees above. Light streamed through an opening in the ceiling farther into the room, and Amaya leaned toward it. This caused her to bump into Belryus, who stomped on Amaya's foot in response.

Amaya gritted her teeth and limped forward, trying to keep the same pace as Vidarr.

Thousands of tuigseach sat in stadium-like seating made of stone, roots, and soil. Each row varied in height and depth, with the lowest tiers taller and deeper. Most of the Ddraigon Kin and Glowers sat in those lower tiers, but some sat higher up. On the far side of the room, two wide staircases led to a single tier of seats, occupied by dozens of tuigseach. Their silver robes carried a symbol of a Neutral Zone planet or station. The one in the center sat in a chair composed entirely of tree roots. This central figure was a Dryadarian with gold and brown leaves instead of hair and wore a large, silver pendant shaped in the form of a tree.

Vidarr held up his fist, and the group paused by the bottom of the stairs. In a whisper, he addressed Amaya, Sol, and Belryus. "Birk Glowfire is a Dryadarian, but he is also the Branch of Cheleth. Remember this. The others, as you can assess, are representatives from every planet in the Neutral Zone Alliance. You will treat them with respect."

"Yes, sir," Amaya said.

Sol and Belryus merely nodded. No one else in their group said anything.

Vidarr's mouth quirked up in a smile as he

nodded to Amaya. "We will move forward now. Follow my lead."

As they walked into the center of the room, Amaya remembered the lessons on presentation and respect her parents had given her, so she pushed her shoulders back, dropped Sol's hand, and stood as tall as she could. Good posture could make her appear more confident, even if she was nervous. If she were the Rayatana, then she had to stand tall and firm as the bringer of peace to The Great Galaxy. Even if she doubted her role, she had to lean into it here. Their trial depended on it.

Vidarr led them into the center of the large beam of light. The Chelethian Security Team spread out into a loose group around them. Vidarr raised his hand and began addressing the crowd by swiveling as he spoke.

"I have brought these for trial for the breaking of our peace, a breaking of the Neutral Zone Agreement."

The crowd, which had been restless when they first arrived, grew silent and somber. Amaya spotted small children gazing down at her with as much solemnity as their parents. She tried to meet their gazes, tried to look as she should as a leader of peace, and was glad that her powers were dampened. She didn't want her emotions running rampant and causing problems. Briefly, she closed her eyes, tipped her head forward, and prayed.

THE JUDGES

The central figure with the silver tree pendant raised a wooden staff and pointed it at the group. "I am Birk Glowfire, Branch of Cheleth and Member of the Neutral Zone Council. You have broken the Neutral Zone Agreement. All but one of you represents a people group responsible for keeping the peace in the Neutral Zone. I ask you to separate yourselves by group and state your plea when called upon."

The Terrs formed ranks in neat rows behind Belryus.

Amaya stood still as Sol took a half-step behind her, showing her status as the leader.

The people in the stands murmured.

Birk Glowfire raised his staff again, and silence fell over the arena. "I see a group of Terr, and a Terr and the unknown entity. Please state the meaning of this."

Amaya stepped forward, but Judge Primus slammed his staff to the ground. "I will hear from

Tanwen Ddraigon Kin first. Where is she?"

Amaya's cheeks blazed, and she was doubly glad her power was contained.

The tuigseach in the stands rustled.

Fingers pointed at her.

"Breathe. Pray. Center," Sol whispered.

She glanced at him, and then down at her hands. She was glowing.

Birk Glowfire leaned forward and pointed his staff at Vidarr. "Vidarr, you have used the Power-Net?"

"Yes, Branch of Cheleth. She is" — Vidarr glanced at a device in his hands — "overpowering it."

The murmurs rose.

Amaya's anger shifted to surprise, and then to amusement at the shock on the judge's face. However satisfying it was, though, she didn't want to create an incident, so she focused on her calming exercises. With every breath, she wound the power deeper in her core. Her skin returned to its normal sienna tone. She also noticed the pain from the power dampener had receded. Was her power strengthening her against it?

Birk Glowfire scowled down at her, and then addressed Vidarr again. "Where is Tanwen?

Vidarr bowed slightly, and said, "There was trouble in the market. Citra took in a Ratterran to ensure her health for the Trial. Tanwen is with her, as well."

Birk's face tightened, and his knuckles grew white around the staff he held. Behind him, the chair of roots writhed, and one of the roots reached out to rest on his shoulder. He slapped it away.

Gasps of surprise echoed in the chamber.

Birk glanced around before sitting allowing the roots to embrace him. Several entered his skin along his arms, and he relaxed slightly, although his lips were pursed in a sour expression.

"Please bring Citra to the Chamber."

"I am here." Citra came forward from the back of the room with Bay and Tanwen. With every step, Citra exuded grace, as if she were dancing, not walking. Citra gave a short nod to Amaya and stepped forward to address the judge.

"This one" —she waved one of her tentacles at Amaya— "is the Rayatana." Citra paused as the stadium erupted into conversations and gasps, even among the Judicial Leaders.

Birk merely raised a leafy eyebrow.

Citra waited a moment before raising her fin-like tentacles so that they wafted around her like tattered, glowing robes. When most of the room had quieted down, she spoke again. "Amaya Iris Benson is Terr, Ratterran, and Earther in heritage."

Amaya's mouth dropped open in shock, but she closed it quickly.

Citra continued. "Amaya was taken from her home by accident, hunted here by the Ratterrans, and forced into taking lives in self-defense. She killed the Nardel through misunderstanding. She is not our enemy, nor the enemy of the Neutral Zone Word and Bond Agreement. She is a child of war, of love, and of chance. As I have seen, and as I have confirmed with the statements of these two witnesses, Tanwen and Bay, a Ratterran. Amaya is the Rayatana."

Rumbling whispers and voices sounded around the arena at her pronouncement.

The Judiciary Council talked among themselves.

Birk steepled his fingers and stared at Citra, and then at Amaya.

Amaya didn't know how much time passed, but it felt like every minute held an age. Her power pushed against the net. She tried to breathe, pray, and center.

Finally, Birk leaned forward.

"Three questions. The first is for Tanwen." He pointed at Tanwen with the staff. "Do you think Amaya Iris Benson is the Rayatana?"

Tanwen lifted her chin. "Amaya Iris Benson is the Rayatana. She is the reason I trained for so many years, so that I may pass my knowledge on to her."

The area grew quiet and still.

Birk brushed one of the roots from his chair away from him, standing up again. "You believe this, truly?"

Tanwen dipped her chin. "Yes."

Birk stepped to the edge of his dais. "The second question is for Amaya. Have you used your power for good or for ill?"

Amaya took a shallow breath, and then a deeper one. Her mouth was dry. She tried to swallow. Her power surged and dimmed. She forced herself to step forward. "I did not know I had power. I do not know how to use it. I used it on my mother in anger, and I regret it. Tanwen has since been training me, but if there is no other way, I would ask if you could design a dampener for me?"

Birk scowled at her. "You admit to misusing the power. You have no training in near adulthood. Yet, you wish to have a dampener. You are unlike any other Rayatana Candidate I have met. But"—he shook his head— "I am not convinced."

Citra's glow changed, brightening to orange.

Birk fixed his gaze on the others. "There is more to be sorted out here." He pointed his staff at Belryus. "The final question is for you, Terr Scout Captain. Why did you come here?"

Belryus stood even straighter and stiffer than she had been. "I am here on the honor of the Terr Protectorate, to apprehend the traitors of our people and return them to Terr."

"The Neutral Zone is a refuge respected by all.

What gives you the right to break into this refuge?"

Belryus glanced over at Sol, and her eyes narrowed in fury. "Sol, cousin to our Prince, has betrayed us. It is a special circumstance."

Birk glanced at the rest of the Neutral Zone Judiciary Representatives. "We need to confer, but I believe refuge in the Neutral Zone is for every single tuigseach, not only the common-born or the unwanted."

Belryus smacked a fist against one of her palms, in a symbolic gesture Amaya didn't recognize. The others seemed to, however. The Chelethian Security Team focused their attention on her as she spoke. "Queen Calanthe sent me personally to take care of this family matter. Surely, you agree that family matters rank above political ones."

Birk rapped his staff against the dais. "In a family as political as the Terr Royal Family, I would say there is no such thing as a non-political family matter. Sol Terr stays on Cheleth. The Neutral Zone Judiciary Representatives and I will confer on your punishment."

Birk returned to his seat and a shield of shimmering power went up between the Neutral Zone Judiciary Representatives and the rest of the room.

The rest of the arena broke into side conversations among the spectators.

Amaya glanced at Sol. His head was down. Waves of relief, frustration, and hope poured off him.

She intertwined her fingers in his again, and he gazed at her. His brow furrowed. "I...I'm glad I found you, Amaya."

Belryus snorted loudly and groaned. "I would rather rot in a prison cell than have to listen to this... offal of sea slugs."

Vidarr stepped closer to her. "Stay where you are."

Belryus rolled her eyes, but stilled and stared down at the ground, clenching her jaw.

The shield dropped and Birk rapped his staff on the ground.

"Belryus and the Bel-25 Crew, despite your violent actions, you did not succeed in hurting anyone other than yourselves. Due to this, and our greater concerns today, we offer you safe passage off Cheleth."

Belryus shook her fist at Birk. "I will not leave without Sol Terr in my custody."

Birk flicked his fingers at the top of his staff. "Then I must imprison you for the safety of Cheleth."

The Chelethian Security Team surrounded Belryus and the Terrs. Belryus turned toward Amaya and narrowed her eyes. Then she made a motion with her fingers. The Terrs around her shifted slightly, and some nodded. After a tense moment, Belryus pivoted on her foot and allowed the Chelethian Security Team to escort them out of the arena.

Amaya didn't know what Belryus's signal to her people meant, but it couldn't be good. Waves of anger came from Sol. She squeezed his arm and turned back to Birk Glowfire and the rest of the judges.

Birk was still staring at her, assessing her. Finally, he turned his gaze to Citra. "The Judiciary Representatives and I have decided to go forth with the Trial of Integrity."

Citra's glow brightened, and then deepened into a dark orange hue before shifting back into a soft, creamy color. Her face didn't change expression, but her glow indicated an internal thought process or emotion. She tilted her chin toward Birk and said, "So be it, Branch of Cheleth."

POWER PLAY

Birk's eyes glowed yellow, and the leaves sprouting from his head flashed with a surge of power through their veins as he turned his glower on Vidarr and Narra. "Prepare them."

Citra held up one hand. "I motion for a break. A short time of preparation before the Trial of Integrity begins."

Birk scowled at her. "We are already gathered."

"Is this truly the will of Cheleth?" Citra asked.

Birk stood, and the roots embedded in his skin released him. "You doubt my connection, Citra? You have been offered this honor and could take my place."

Citra's skin glowed purple, and then receded to cream. "I will share the connection with you until the test is finished."

Birk Glowfire's power surged and expanded to light the room, but Citra stepped onto the steps and climbed them to the council's seats.

The crowd murmured.

"What is going on?" Amaya whispered to Tanwen.

Tanwen ran a hand over her chin. "Birk offered Citra his seat, thinking she would refuse as she has every time before, and she's just called his bluff. By taking the seat, she can connect with the planet of Cheleth and Birk, plus have a deciding vote in your favor. It shows her trust in you as the Rayatana."

Amaya leaned toward Tanwen. "What does it mean to connect with Cheleth?"

"Cheleth is not just a planet but a sentient being, a tree and root system holding the planet together."

Amaya turned slowly and took in the sight of the roots which held up the walls of the arena. The roots of Cheleth. And the roots came together in the wide chair where Birk had been seated. The chair quivered and expanded into a seat for Birk and Citra, who towered over him and needed more legroom. Birk's power dimmed, and as he sat, the roots embedded themselves into his arms again. Citra sat beside him. The way the roots enveloped her and her tentacles entwined with them, it was as if she became part of the root system, except for her proud head and dark, wide eyes fixated on the arena floor.

Amaya didn't understand half of what was

going on, but she didn't want to let Citra down. As she held Citra's gaze, she wondered again what it meant to be the Rayatana when a powerful being like Citra expected so much of her.

BY ROOT AND WIRE

Sol put a hand on her shoulder and squeezed it just as a group of green-clad tuigseach came toward them. They appeared wary of Amaya, but after a moment, one of them approached her, a Dryadarian-Glower with red leaves mixed with reddish-brown hair and blue-green glowing skin.

"I am Lumien, son of Citra Gia of the Glower Margos, and I will help you connect to Cheleth. I apologize for any discomfort ahead of time."

Amaya bowed her head slightly, keeping her eyes on him. "I am honored to meet the son of Citra Gia of the Glower Margos."

He lowered his chin slightly, and a tiny smile quirked the edge of his lips. "And I am honored to meet the Rayatana. We have long awaited your coming."

Fibrous roots and electrical wiring lowered from the ceiling, and the Chelethian Security Team stepped back. Vidarr stood nearby, but Sol was ushered a few feet away from Amaya by another green-clad tuigseach.

Lumien took a bundle of roots and wire and plugged them into something that looked like an electrode patch. "I'll be attaching nodes to each point indicated by the holes in your clothes." He knelt down by her leg. "Are you ready?"

Amaya glanced nervously at the others. Sol, Bay, and Tanwen were having the patches attached to their legs, arms, and the base of their skulls.

"Um, may I ask, why root and wire?"

"Cheleth will watch the trial, as well as the council," Lumien said. He held out the patch to show it to her.

She didn't understand the technology being used, but she nodded her agreement and waited. While he attached one of the patches to her right leg, she squeezed her hands together in front of her. The patch attached to her with a sticky substance, which was warm on contact. A tiny tickle of sensation came after that. Amaya tensed, but nothing else happened.

"No pain, just a small sensation?" Lumien asked her.

She nodded; not sure she could speak through a suddenly dry throat.

He affixed three more electrodes to her — her other leg and her forearms.

"So, Cheleth, the tree-plant being? I'm attached

to its roots now? Will it speak to me?"

Lumien paused and cocked his head at her, as if studying her. "You are very brave to undergo such a joining without being familiar with this." He held up one of the patches to show her the tiny roots and electrical wires poking through the side he would attach to her. "I am a Dryadarian, so this is familiar to me. I can"—he paused and held up his other hand—"grow rootlets from my skin to attach to others or to the soil, or to a machine." As he spoke, tiny rootlets poked out of his skin and receded.

Amaya swallowed back a bit of nauseous fear. "Um, okay. But how does Cheleth communicate?"

He held out his hand, and she placed her hand tentatively in his. One tiny rootlet grew out of his hand and touched the side of hers. It felt like the brush of a cat's fur, even as it sank into her skin. Suddenly, she wasn't alone in her own skin. The presence of Lumien was somehow part of her. She couldn't hear his thoughts or feel his emotions exactly, but it was like she could hear and feel the echo of them. A tiny voice came out of the echo.

"It is difficult to speak this way. Cheleth is more powerful but cherishes all life." The tiny echoing whisper faded, and Lumien dropped her hand. No mark remained from where the rootlet had been. Her skin closed.

Amaya stared at him and the patch he held,

suddenly aware of each patch attached to her. "Why am I not feeling Cheleth yet?"

"Cheleth will wait until the Trial of Integrity begins to interact with you. Part of the process involves an interactive computer simulation. Cheleth will not control that part but will be with you in the process."

Amaya took a shaky breath, her skin beginning to glow.

Lumien held out the patch. "Cheleth will keep you safe."

"Okay, I guess. I need to do this." Amaya took another breath, counted to three, and let it out slowly.

He nodded and reached back to affix the last electrode-root patch to the back of her neck. It didn't feel any different than the other patches, and she stood still as he attached the rest. When he was finished, he handed her a pair of goggles.

"These will help ease the transition into the simulation."

She put them on, and the room took on a greenish tinge. "When will it begin?"

He waved his hand upward. "When the roots lift you."

At this strange statement, he walked away.

As he did, the power dampeners eased, like the lifting of a weight from her shoulders. When the dampeners lifted, she fully embraced her power, and it diffused through her. Her hands glowed faintly, but she was in control, allowing the power to give her strength to help her remain calm.

Through her goggles, she gazed around the room. The others were all similarly outfitted, and then four more roots dropped from the ceiling. One encircled her like a harness. The other roots did the same to Tanwen, Sol, and Bay. She sensed Sol fighting anxiety. Or was he fighting her anxiety? She didn't know. The roots lifted them, her goggles went dark, and then bright again.

An image superimposed over the room—an image of a ruined temple in a desert. Her feet dangled in the air of the testing center and rested on solid ground. Her clothes were her trial uniform and a black form-fitting uniform complete with a utility belt.

She staggered in the sand; the two images making her dizzy. Was she suspended or on solid ground? She felt both, saw both, and then...

Sol took her hand. She concentrated on his emotions—his confidence buoying hers.

They were standing on a dune, above a ruined desert temple. Beside them, Bay floundered in the sand.

Amaya held out her hand. "Bay, we're here."

Bay took Amaya's hand with trembling fingers. "I...I've never done this before."

"Focus on us. On the simulation," Sol said. He also held out a hand.

Bay ignored it. She studied Tanwen, instead, who stood straight and stared at the temple below.

Tanwen pointed to the temple. "That's our first objective. I don't know what we'll find there, but that's where we go, but let's go slowly. There may be traps, and we can find our feet."

"Will you lead us?" Amaya asked.

"Under your command," Tanwen said and began walking down the steep slope.

SINKING SANDS

Following Tanwen down the giant dune, Amaya wondered what her real body was doing outside the simulation. As the thought crossed her mind, she caught a glimpse of the council chamber, from where she dangled in the air, and she stumbled forward in the sand, rolling head over heels for several feet before coming to a stop.

She had released Bay's and Sol's hands when she'd fallen, and they were struggling to stay upright on the dune. She lay still for a moment, feeling the sand slithering through her clothes, gritty against her skin. It wasn't real, but it felt real.

Again, she blinked and saw the testing chamber, with the council members seated nearly even with where she dangled in the air. She concentrated on the grit of the sand, the heat of the sun, the slope of the dune, and on the sounds of the others' voices as they walked carefully toward her, their feet sinking with every step.

When she felt more focused on the simulation, she sat up, rolled to her toes, and stood. Getting her feet under her felt good, and she took a step down the slope, before turning to wait for the others. Focusing on the simulation required a certain amount of concentration. She wasn't sure if they could get lost in it.

When the others reached her, Sol held out a hand, and Bay held out another. "Do you want us to anchor you?"

She didn't think she needed it but thought their show of working together was good, so she accepted their hands, and they continued down the slope. Tanwen stayed a step or two in front.

"I imagine there will be a challenge, a test, a riddle, or something to find when we get to the temple. There usually is."

The sand dragged at Amaya's feet, but she kept moving forward with the others. "How many of these have you been in?"

Tanwen shrugged. "I was trained in them when my parents thought I was the Rayatana. Ddraigon Kin live longer than others do, so I am expected to live around four hundred years, possibly more. The first hundred years are considered a training time, the second are for discovery or further training. I'm one-hundred-and fifty. I stopped training seventeen years ago, but I trained from the age of thirty to one-hundred-and-twenty in the simulation modules every week at first, and then once a month. I refused for a while. They weren't teaching me anything new anymore."

"So, we should follow your lead," Sol said.

"Or subvert it? Remember, I didn't become the Rayatana," Tanwen said.

"And do you mind that?" Bay asked.

The thought was on Amaya's mind as well, she wasn't sure if she could train for something so long and be all right with losing it.

"I did, for a time. But even in the thick of it, even as a child, I doubted they had the right person. It wore at me. The worry. I was too prone to melancholy and odd moments of humor, fits of high energy. It wasn't until after I was formally released from the title of Rayatana Candidate that I found the help I needed to accept who I am."

"And you are what?" Amaya asked.

Tanwen laughed. "Your mentor. Your advisor. Your help. Plus, I am" — she frowned — "a woman with what you on Earth call depression. I must monitor my vital signs. There are training methods I use for my mind to help me, but there are days it is best I am quiet. The beauty and oddness of having what I have and being who I am, I have an ongoing illness of the mind, but also the means to heal it myself, as long as I pay attention. I keep a log." She touched her wrist, and an embedded chip flared to life, revealing several graphs, all glowing green. "Currently, I am well." She tapped the chip again, and it receded. Her arm once again appeared bare.

"That's fifth-generation med-tech," Bay said, shaking her head in awe. "That's impressive. My father never even knew you had it. Or is it only visible in the simulation?"

"I didn't use it on your ship." Tanwen slid her gaze over to Amaya and then at the temple they were approaching. "Because of this new information you have about me, I understand if you do not wish me to remain your advisor."

Amaya almost responded with quick assurance, but that wouldn't be fair. She considered what she knew of Tanwen, of her history, of her condition, and the device she had in her arm. "Keep me updated. You've given me sound advice. I will not always take every bit of advice, because I must make my own choices, but I will listen. Does that work?"

"Yes," Tanwen said.

"I would like to know more about the technology of the device. Is it photo-medicine?" Sol asked.

"No."

"Not exactly."

Tanwen and Bay looked at each other.

Bay rushed in with an explanation. "It utilizes photo-medicine technology, but it uses the power of the bearer to maintain itself when light is unavailable. The tech can be used by those with the gift, and there are many types of devices, some for monitory and some for prosthesis of various kinds."

"And a Ratterran gunner knows this because…?" Sol quirked his eyebrow up, but his jaw tensed.

Bay lifted her chin and dropped Amaya's hand. "That's my business."

Amaya sensed something deeper there and felt the flare of Sol's curiosity. "We can discuss it at a later time if we need to, until then, we're here." She pointed at the temple steps ahead of them. She wondered for a flicker of a moment if they had really walked the length of the dune or if the simulation had hurried them along. It appeared — she caught a glimpse of the testing arena, and then focused on the sun beating down on her — as though the simulation had shortened their trip. She focused on the feel of Sol's hand in hers, how Bay shielded her eyes to stare at the temple, and the way Tanwen climbed the first few steps to inspect a carving on one of the stone pillars.

"We should stick together," Amaya said.

The ground shifted, Tanwen stumbled on the stone steps.

"Get to Tanwen!" Amaya ran forward, tugging Sol along with her.

Bay heard, saw what she meant, and leapt onto

the stone steps a half-step behind Amaya. She charged up the staircase to Tanwen with short powerful strides and took a hold of Tanwen's shoulder.

Amaya and Sol came to stand on the other side of Tanwen.

"The temple is sinking!" Sol shouted.

"I need to decipher this text," Tanwen said. "Then we should get inside."

Amaya glanced at the carvings in a language she hadn't seen before.

Tanwen continued to translate, muttering to herself while she did so. "Sinking sands, desolate lands…all must fall…all must…ruin…until the temple…rises with the…"

Amaya watched the lower steps sink behind the sand. The sand rose quickly. She wanted to hurry Tanwen but knew it wouldn't work to jostle her concentration. She didn't want to fail now when they'd just started.

"Rises with the…star…sun…no…light? Light life?"

The sand rose to the step beneath them.

"We have to go," Bay shouted.

Tanwen glanced back, nodded. "Close enough. Let's get inside."

They ran into the temple together. The sand

poured up the last steps, rushing after them like a wave. Under the portico, a single narrow door was open on the back wall. They rushed toward it. Amaya went first, pulling Sol after her. Tanwen made a garbled protest as Bay pushed her in before shutting the door.

IN THE TEMPLE

Darkness descended.

Sand whooshed against the door.

Tanwen's skin lit up, and Bay held up her finger, now glowing, to create a double circle of light around their group.

The door held against the sand, but the sand poured through the cracks around it.

The space around them felt hollow and solid, cavernous and present.

Tanwen glowed stronger, revealing a row of pillars in what resembled a grand entryway, a mirror of the portico outside, but with stone surrounding them.

The rushing sound of shifting sand against the door outside slowed to a trickle.

"We move forward, always." Tanwen held out one glowing hand and let the rest of her skin subside to its normal pale coloring.

Bay continued to hold up her glowing finger.

Sol's eyes glowed green in the darkness, but not enough to do more than light up his face in a way that could have been eerie but highlighted his handsome features.

Amaya reached out to twine her fingers with his again. "Forward."

Tanwen led them into the hall, and they stayed in a tight-knit group.

The pillars appeared endless, but then an animal's roar came from their right, and a trumpeting sound came from their left.

"Run!" Tanwen jogged forward.

Amaya and the others stayed with her, pressing deeper into the cavernous hall.

The roaring grew nearer, to the right and slightly behind. The trumpeting combined with heavy footsteps on their left, and behind them.

"There's a door. We're being herded," Tanwen said. She slowed and came to a stop in front of a stone door with an ornate handle.

Amaya and the others stopped, too. "Why aren't we going through the door?" she asked.

"It could be a trap. It's almost too easy." Tanwen knelt door to peer closely at the handle, which had the head of a Nardel, all teeth and spiky hair, and the legs of some other animal with huge feet and blunt talons.

"We know what's behind us. I think we should open it," Sol said.

"It might separate us." Tanwen fingered the crease where the two different creatures came together. "These creatures don't go naturally together."

"Let's hold hands then." Amaya held out her free hand to Bay.

Bay took it.

Tanwen took one of Bay's hands, and then she opened the door.

Amaya couldn't see anything on the other side, not even Tanwen's light penetrated the darkness, but a heavy pull of energy came from the door, tugging at Tanwen, until they all stumbled forward, falling.

Falling…falling…falling…

Amaya had screamed once before remembering the simulation. For a moment, she caught the flicker of the testing chamber, and then she was back, falling… falling…falling…

She gripped Sol's and Bay's hands in her own. Sol squeezed her hand with assurance, but Bay's hand felt slippery in her grasp. Bay's fingers flexed around hers, but in the next moment, Bay slipped away in the darkness.

"No! Bay's gone!"

"Tanwen, too." Sol gripped her hand even tighter.

"Give me your other hand." Amaya tried to pull against their joined hands to maneuver in the free fall, but his hand slipped out of hers.

"Sol!"

"Remember, Amaya, I'm here. Even if you can't see me." Sol's voice echoed up to her as he fell away.

Amaya continued to fall into the darkness. Falling…falling…falling…but she knew it wasn't real. She could feel Sol's presence through their Zoe Bond. Nothing could break it. Except for death. And they weren't going to die in a simulation. Or at least she didn't think they could.

Amaya relaxed as Sol's calm assurance, his confidence, and his arrogance came through the Zoe Bond. She smiled. Of course, he would be arrogant in the middle of this test.

PLATFORMS

She relaxed, the sensation of falling dissipated, and she found herself standing on an oval platform above a dark abyss. To the right, a raised platform of three conjoined stars lit up. To the left, a lowered platform in the shape of a shooting star with a tail brightened. In front of her, an oval raised platform with a jagged line shone.

Sol stood on the platform of three conjoined star shapes, the symbol of the Terr Protectorate. Bay prowled the edge of the shooting star platform, the symbol of the Ratterran Alliance, and Tanwen knelt on the oval with the jagged line, which Amaya didn't know the meaning of.

A disembodied voice came from all around them.

"One. Four. Many."

Several platforms surrounding Amaya began to glow, stretching out into a deep, dark horizon.

"Only one platform may rise."

Tanwen's lips moved, and she waved her hands frantically.

Amaya couldn't hear her. The sound between the platforms was missing, as if they were each in their own chamber, although she could see everyone clearly.

Bay paced on her platform.

Sol sat, cross-legged, and nodded to Amaya. His trust and affirmation radiated from him.

"You have limited time." The voice spoke again.

A cube rose on Amaya's platform. It opened to reveal four items: a grenjen, a set of ropes, a device that looked like a high-tech grappling hook, and a communicator.

"You may choose two items."

Amaya didn't hesitate. She pulled out the ropes and the grappler.

Sol nodded and gathered the same items. Tanwen had done the same.

But Bay had a grenjen and a grappler. What was she thinking?

It didn't matter. Amaya had to trust her instincts. This wasn't a test of one person's ability to reach the top, but the test of a person's ability to lead. Even if Bay hadn't followed her, she could still bring her along, and to do that, she shot her grappler at Bay's platform.

Bay pointed her grenjen at Amaya. When the hook hit the edge of her platform, she dropped the weapon.

After hooking the grappler base on her platform, she prepared to take the rope across. The climbing gear had a simple harness with a sturdy ascender to help her stop. Extra rope and clips were a part of the gear. Carefully, Amaya threw the rope over her shoulder, with the clips situated in a way she could reach them. She sat on the platform and scooted forward until her feet dangled off the side. She clenched the grappler base. Her chest tightened, and she took one shaky breath. She was too scared.

She huffed out the air and stared at the horizon.

"Time is limited," the disembodied voice stated.

Amaya breathed deep into her stomach and let out the air slowly. She took a carabiner clip and attached it to her harness. Clipping another one, she slipped a loop of rope around the rope between the platforms, and knotted it. One breath in. Knot checked. Another breath. Clip to rope.

It was time. Everything was clipped in. She had created an extra safety rope. She had checked the knot on it. Her clips would hold. Inhaling again, she hooked one leg over the rope.

Taking hold of the rope with her hands, she pulled herself out over the edge. A whimper escaped her lips as she swung from the rope. She tried to pray, but her mind was jumbled in panic.

The rope bit into her clenched fingers.

"Please, please," she whispered. With her teeth gritted, she hooked her other leg over the rope so she hung upside down.

"Please." Her arms trembled, but she took one deep breath and reached one hand out over her head for the rope. When she had a good handhold, she moved her other hand up and over, and slid her legs toward her arms. The carabiner clips held her weight easily, and she slid across the strong climbing rope. Fear had its hooks in her, but she focused on her breathing. With every slow intake of breath, she moved one hand, and then the other, forward on the rope. With every exhale, she slid her legs forward.

As she inched away from her platform toward Bay's platform, the ache in her arms grew with every pull. Her fingers had hardened into painful claws. Her legs grew sore. Fixing her gaze on the rope in front of her, she made herself keep going. "One more. Just one more." She whispered the words.

Finally, when she reached her hand over her head, it bumped into Bay's platform.

Her throat tightened. Tears sprang to her eyes.

Bay leaned over the edge of her platform. "I've got you."

When Amaya's head was next to Bay's platform,

Bay put her hands under Amaya's shoulders and lifted her up.

Bay sat down next to her. "I'm sorry. I didn't even think of…joining forces."

Amaya waved her hand upward. "They said, 'Only one platform may rise,' which means that we don't climb out, we find a way to get this thing to go up."

"Oh." Bay sighed. "I guess that's why I'm not you." She held out the grenjen. "Do you want to take it?"

"No. It's okay. I always need someone to guard my back." Amaya held out a balled fist to Bay. "Are we good?"

"Um, yeah." Bay stared at Amaya's hand.

Amaya kept her fist up. "It's like an Earther oath shake. Make a fist and tap your knuckles against mine."

As they finished the fist bump, Tanwen climbed onto the platform. She had followed Amaya's lead.

Amaya went to give her a hand as Tanwen unclipped her harness.

"You figured it out, I think," Tanwen said.

"I hope so."

A thump from the other side of the platform told them Sol had made it.

As he struggled to climb onto the platform, Bay

walked over to him.

Amaya watched as Bay held out her hand.

Sol took it, and she pulled him the rest of the way up.

"Now, how do we get this thing to rise?" Amaya asked.

The simulation blinked around them.

For a moment, Amaya stood in the arena on Cheleth.

A huge boom and a hard shake made her stumble on her feet.

The simulation blinked back into focus. They were still on the platform.

BLINK

"What happened?"

Another blink and they stood in the arena. People in the stands were vacating their seats, scrambling for the exit.

Sol reached to disconnect himself from the testing apparatus.

Another blip, and they stood in the simulation.

"Get unhooked!" Tanwen shouted.

Blip. They were in the arena.

Amaya reached for the connection at the back of her neck. She pulled, and it came out with wrenching pain. The other cables and roots tightened, then relaxed, and she fell to the floor. The roots pulled from her skin, wound around the cables, and pulled them out as well. Nausea welled up in her, and she spit bile out onto the floor.

Yanking her goggle off, she struggled to stand

upright.

Around her, the arena roared in chaos. People were shouting and running. Citra, the Glower, stood at the top of the stands. Power encircled her and those around her in a shielded bubble. Birk Glowfire was not visible. Grenjens, and something that looked like a cannon attached to the arms of the attackers, shot into the chamber. Citra's bubble held, but she gazed down at Amaya and pointed at the arena.

Amaya went to Sol, who knelt on the ground, breathing hard.

He waved her away. "I'm all right. Help Bay."

She went to Bay, who was trapped in the simulation. Her eyes stared at something Amaya couldn't see. Amaya reached for the cord at her neck.

Tanwen grabbed her wrist. "No! She might not wake up. Wait for the next blip."

A blast from a weapon hit the ground next to them.

Amaya flinched away but stayed close to Bay.

Someone shouted at her from across the room.

Bay gasped and stared at Amaya.

Amaya wrenched the connection from Bay's neck, and Bay collapsed onto her, dragging her to the floor.

A shot fired over their heads and hit the cables

and roots Bay had been connected to.

Tanwen's hands glowed with pure power, bright blue and yellow mixed with green tendrils. "I'll cover you. Get to the judge's stands."

Amaya hauled Bay toward the stands. When they reached the lower stand, they ducked behind it.

"I don't have enough power to do more than sting someone who gets close to me. I can't do what Tanwen's doing, or what you can do," Bay told Amaya.

They watched Tanwen throw her power at the attackers in streaks of green energy that knocked them off their feet and sent their suits of armor into an electric storm.

"I don't know how to do that. I…could kill us," Amaya said.

"You have it under control," Bay said. "Otherwise, you'd have already blown something up."

Amaya chuckled. "I guess you're right. I don't even know why that's funny, but it is." She took a shaky breath. "It gets out of control when I'm angry, and I'm terrified."

"So, I don't think you should get really angry, but imagine how badly the people of this planet are getting hurt. Doesn't that…make you want to change what's going on here, stand up for them?"

"Yes." Fierce heat built up in Amaya's core. "Stay behind me."

"I've got your back."

"Thanks."

Amaya held her power back and searched for the right opportunity to use it.

Sol was across from them, fighting an attacker hand to hand. She couldn't help him, and through their Bond, she sensed his confidence. He would be all right.

Tanwen stood in the center of the room, directing her energy in controlled bursts at individual attackers.

Amaya stretched out her hands in the direction of the doorway, where a group of attackers prepared a device. She poured her power through her hands. Golden light streaked out of her, mixed with shades of red and blue, becoming a golden-purple stream that went right at the attackers and their device. The device exploded with a loud whoom sound, causing the doorway to collapse.

Amaya closed her hands, hoping she could stop the power from hitting anyone else.

The power encircled her knuckles, glowing and writhing. Heat built behind her eyes.

"I don't know if I can control it." She squeezed her eyelids shut.

COLLAPSE

Amaya took in a long, deep breath. Just one word came to her mind in prayer. "Please."

She opened her eyes to stare at her hands. They were still glowing, but it was a softer glow.

"Good. You're mastering it," Bay said.

Amaya glanced around the room.

Sol stood over the soldier he had fought, taking off the attacker's helmet.

Tanwen blasted one last attacker and stopped. She swayed on her feet.

Amaya went to her and threw an arm around her.

"You did it," Tanwen said, with a small smile. "I knew you could." She held out her hand. "If you can, push some of your energy into my hand, and I will renew myself."

Amaya put her hand over Tanwen's and gave

her power a nudge. A small, warm part of the glow settled over Tanwen's hand, and she breathed out in relief. "Thank you. That's enough. You may be able to help me heal the injured."

A loud boom shook the roof over their heads.

"Or she may need to fight more with it," Bay said, coming to stand beside them.

Sol joined them. He radiated sadness and anger.

Amaya focused inward. She held onto her sense of self. The sadness and anger from Sol lessened. Had she exerted control over their Zoe Bond? She didn't think that was possible, but she didn't say anything to the others.

Sol held out a communicator with Terr insignia on it. "I will never call myself Terr again."

"They attacked a neutral planet," Bay said, her tone grim. "That is cause for war."

"Aren't you already at war?" Amaya asked.

"We have been holding back," Bay said. "The Ratterran Allied Forces will not hold back any longer, not when they hear of this."

"Not only that, but the Neutral Zone Treaty Planets will band together and form their force," Tanwen stated. "They will not fight directly with the Ratterrans, but they will aid them in the common cause, to force the Terrs to suffer the consequences for their actions here."

Another boom shook the roof.

Citra, who had kept her bubble of power around her and the others huddled inside of it, dropped it to speak. "We need to leave this chamber, quickly. The roots of Cheleth are strained. If you come up to the stands, I can create a way for us."

Another boom hit overhead. Around them, the roots shifted, and the chamber walls started to crumble.

"Let's go."

Tanwen glanced around the room. "I think someone is alive over there."

A mound of bodies shifted. From underneath them, Narra stood, shoving them away. "I need help over here. Lumien is down." She helped the Dryadarian technician to his feet.

"Coming." Sol ran over to them, with Bay close behind him.

"Thank you," Lumien said, as Bay put her arm around his waist and helped him balance on his feet.

The ceiling trembled, and rocks fell around them.

Tanwen's eyes glowed, and her voice dropped. "When the planets of the…"

Amaya interrupted Tanwen by grabbing her arm. "Let's be all serious and vision-y later. We need to get out of here."

Tanwen blinked and stumbled, but she regained her footing and followed Amaya up the stairs. Sol, Bay, and Narra half-carried Lumien up the stairs.

Citra had extended her shield of power again. Instead of a bubble, it was an umbrella, keeping the falling rocks from landing on their heads. A huge boulder came down, and Amaya cringed, but the umbrella shield held, and the boulder fell to the side.

Citra waved to a large root on the wall to her right. "This one leads up to the surface. We will follow it." She reached out a hand and placed it on the root. A small tunnel formed alongside the root, with its sides held apart by Citra's power.

Several of the testers and council members who had been saved by Citra in the attack started crawling into the tunnel.

"Can we help you?" Tanwen asked Citra.

Citra smiled. "Save your strength for the fight."

Bay knelt and got into the tunnel. "How will we help Lumien up this?"

"Amaya, if you will?" Tanwen reached out a trembling hand and held it over Lumien.

Amaya put her hand over Tanwen's and focused on creating a soft glow of energy. Then she pushed her power gently into Tanwen's hand, and Tanwen directed the energy into Lumien. The wound on his forehead started to knit together.

He gasped and reached for Citra. "Mom, if you bond with Cheleth…"

"I know, son. We spoke of this." Citra's appendages flowed over Lumien and wrapped around his shoulders. He hugged her close as tears ran down his face.

When Lumien let go of his mom, the roots of Cheleth wound around her, and she became a glowing force that lit up the roots on the sides of the tunnel they needed to escape.

Tanwen went into the tunnel, followed by Bay.

Sol crawled into the tunnel next, and said, "Amaya?"

"I'm coming." She gazed at Citra's face, still visible within the roots. "Will you make it out?"

Citra smiled again. "Yes, but as a Glower, my life and Cheleth's will be forever intertwined. I don't have time to explain, except to say it is my choice, and you must honor it."

Amaya put a hand to her heart and bowed her head to Citra. "Thank you."

"Go."

Amaya crawled into the tunnel, with Lumien right behind her.

The tunnel began to collapse. The ground rumbled in waves.

20

FIGHT FOR THE SURFACE

The mad scramble through the tunnel seemed to last forever and mere seconds at the same time. Citra's power energized the roots around the tunnel with light, which showed their way in a web of color and structure. They climbed and climbed, and finally, they exited into the wide entry chamber. As they huddled outside the tunnel entrance, roots formed around the doorway and sank into the floor. The glow dissipated.

Amaya touched one of the root-frames of the doorway gently and noticed Lumien curling his fingers around the other side. "I'm sorry, Lumien."

"It is…what she saw before, that Cheleth would have need of her." He leaned his forehead against the door frame. "I know I will see her again, but she will be changed."

An explosion rocked the courtyard, and debris rained around them.

"That's a ship-based weapon," Sol said. "We

can't fight those from the ground."

Amaya touched Lumien's arm briefly before facing the others. "Let's get out of this building and find out what we're up against."

"We need to get to our ships," Bay said. "I haven't seen my dad since I came off the simulation, and I know that's where he would go."

"No." Narra held up her hand. "Cheleth has a security system. I am not sure why it hasn't been activated, but Lumien and I can do that from the library."

"You have weapon controls in the library?" Amaya asked.

"Knowledge is power," Lumien said. It was a trite statement, but his words were tinged with sadness.

Amaya hadn't known Citra for more than fleeting minutes, but the Glower had stood up for her, and she could imagine what Lumien felt. She didn't even know if her mom was safe in the theater-spaceship, or if she'd been taken captive by the Terr Protectorate.

Sol reached out to hold her hand. She twined her fingers with his, comforted by his physical touch and the assurance flowing from him, but beneath it all, she felt his sorrow and smoldering anger at his people for the attack.

She nodded. "Take us there."

"Follow me." Lumien set a brisk pace through

the courtyard, avoiding the falling rubble.

Bay, Tanwen, Sol, and Amaya followed Lumien in a tight pack, with Narra taking a rear-guard position. When Amaya glanced back, she saw Narra sweeping the area with her gaze.

Amaya scrutinized the fallen columns, the bodies in ones and twos scattered over the broken stones of the walkway, and the holes in the trellis. The Terrs had ruined the place.

Outside the courtyard, Lumien took a sharp left and jogged down the street, staying close to the walls of the buildings.

Amaya and her team stayed in stride with him, even Narra who had to take two steps for every single stride of Lumien's pace.

Amaya glanced back at her again, but Narra shook her head and pointed forward. "Don't waste your time looking out for me. Keep track of yourself and your team. I know my city, my planet, and my abilities."

Amaya's cheeks burned. She should know better. Since when had being shorter than average ever held her back? Why would she think it would be any different for Narra?

Lumien led them down several blocks and took another right into a massive outdoor park with stone paths winding around in a spiral pattern toward a central building encased in the roots of a tree. The tree itself stretched upward so high Amaya couldn't see the top of it, but she could see a hole had been punched through some of the branches on one side. Terr weapons had been at work here.

As a burnt leaf fell from one of the tree's branches, Amaya stopped. The others slowed to a stop, and Lumien looked back at them, somehow sensing that they were no longer with him.

"Cheleth's main trunk, as our world-tree, giver of all knowledge," Lumien said.

A massive explosion hit the ground near them and lifted Amaya into the air. She tried to roll when she hit the ground, but it was clumsy, with the earth shaking and her ears numb from the sound.

Sol's heartbeat pounded steadily through the Zoe Bond.

As she climbed to her feet, she noticed the others moving slowly. Tanwen had shifted into her half-dragon form. Her claws dug into the grass, and her eyes were wild with power.

Amaya tried to get to her, but she stumbled from the aftershocks of another missile strike.

Tanwen glowed brighter. A moment later, her power ebbed, and she shifted back to her humanoid form. She dropped to her knees.

Amaya reached her side. "What happened?"

"My medicine. It's...not working." Tanwen shuddered, and tears rolled down her cheeks. "I can't...I feel..." Tears tracked down her cheeks. "It's too much. I'm..."

"Help!" Bay shrieked from several feet away. One of her legs had gone limp. She had rolled onto her forearms and used one leg and her forearms to crawl.

Lumien ran to her and swept her into his arms. "That bomb had a double effect, taking down any bio-tech, as well as slamming the planet with explosives. We have to get inside. Both Bay's and Tanwen's bio-tech shut off. Bay's prosthetic isn't working, and the sudden lapse of aid is making Tanwen's depression far worse than it would be if she'd weaned off it."

Narra touched Tanwen's forehead. "If you allow me."

"Yes," Tanwen whispered.

Narra pressed her fingertips. They glowed slightly, and Tanwen's eyes went glassy. A second later, she went slack, and Narra lifted her.

Amaya reached out to help, but Narra shook her head. "I may not have your vertical height, but my muscles are three times stronger than other tuigseach. Let's get into the library." She ran with Tanwen over her shoulder.

Lumien followed her, holding Bay.

KNOWLEDGE IS POWER

Lumien kept a brisk pace, but he slowed every few paces to gaze around and swivel his long, pointed ears.

Amaya thought she was used to seeing the various tuigseach, but Lumien had looked so human at first glance, despite the leaves intertwined in his hair and his bright aqua skin. She hadn't seen his lengthy, pointed ears until he had pushed his leafy mane behind them.

Inside the entryway of the library, Lumien crouched and signaled for them to do the same. He rested Bay on the floor gently. She twisted to rest on her knees so she could look around, not even making eye contact with Amaya.

Amaya ducked down near Bay and placed a hand on her shoulder.

In front of them, a huge panel of glass stretched across the library entryway, but the lower half of it was darkened.

Everyone crept forward until they were near the glass and Lumien could whisper to them.

"There's a group of Terr soldiers inside in full tactical gear. I don't see the librarians. The entrance to the inner sanctum is blocked."

Narra huddled next to Lumien. She had laid Tanwen down on the floor. "We'll have to fight our way in."

"There's too many."

"If you combine your power with Sol and Amaya, you can create a shield over the rest of us or surge the Terrs."

Lumien shook his head. "You know…"

"I do. But you need to do this to save Cheleth."

Lumien gave a curt nod. "It is so." He cocked his ears toward Amaya. "Do you know how to join power?"

"I have given some power to Tanwen."

Lumien put one hand over his face. "Dear Triple One…we need you."

"It is so," Narra said.

"It is so," Amaya echoed.

Lumien glanced around at their group.

Amaya shared his concern. Tanwen was in a glassy-eyed state, and Bay couldn't walk. Amaya was half-trained, and Sol was clenching his hands and releasing them, repeatedly.

Lumien placed his hand on the floor, and a tiny root tendril burst through it and wrapped around one of his fingers. Lumien's breath hitched, and then he said, "We will all join."

"I don't have the same kind of power," Narra said.

"Everyone has power."

"That's not… never mind. I'll hold hands with everyone, but I get one hand free for my arm cannon."

"Agreed." Lumien held out a hand to Bay.

Amaya placed her other hand on Tanwen. Sol put his hand on Tanwen's shoulder, then Narra put a hand on his forearm, pointing her arm-cannon toward the doors.

"And we will surge on my count. One, two, three—" Lumien counted up and glanced over the frosted glass. "Four."

Amaya peeked in time to see the Terrs in their battle armor lifting their arm canons.

"Five."

A tentative pull brushed against Amaya's senses and she relaxed, allowing the others to draw power from her and allowing Lumien to direct it.

Their power flared in one, huge, bright surge.

Glass shattered.

Amaya kept her eyes open, although all she could see was light.

The power dimmed.

"Surge again in five."

They did, and the screams of the Terrs in the library told Amaya all she needed to know.

More Terrs came out of the stacks, shouting and drawing their weapons.

Amaya had lost count, but she heard Sol say, "Four, five."

Their combined power surged again, and the world became all light and all sound.

Then silence.

The power dimmed, and they dropped hands.

Lumien lifted Bay gently, Narra took up Tanwen, and everyone walked into the wreckage of the library. Bodies on the floor, stacks toppled over, books everywhere.

"In." Lumien directed them, and Amaya focused on Sol's shoulders.

Sol's grief hit her.

Her own shock echoed it.

The waste of life. The destruction. This was not what she wanted to use her power for, but it was a battle they had to fight to save the planet.

She swallowed down the bile that rose to her throat and tried to send determination through the Zoe Bond to Sol.

Finally, Lumien approached a door. Two Chelethian security guards were down on the floor outside of it, dead.

The sight of all the bodies burned into Amaya's retinas, into her soul.

Lumien waved a hand back at them. "Narra, I need your scan."

Narra placed Tanwen on the ground, and then she bent toward the locking mechanism so her eye could be scanned. Lumien provided a thumbprint.

The door opened, and they hurried into a small chamber where another door with a huge locking mechanism stood.

This one took a combination code. Once through it, Narra closed the door behind them.

The lights came on when they entered. They were in a metal room, surrounded by wall screens. No one else was there.

Lumien and Narra immediately ran to separate consoles.

"Defense mechanisms, locking now."

They each turned a key on their consoles. The lights in the room dimmed, a mechanical hum sounded, and the screens displayed a web of light surrounding the planet. One of the Terr battleships was inside the web, but the rest were outside of it. Missiles pounded against the shield, but they could not break it.

DISCOVERY

With the immediate threat over, Amaya dropped into a chair by one of the consoles. She closed her eyes, trying not to think of the carnage outside this small room.

After a few moments, she opened her eyes again, because she had to check on her people. Sol sat on the ground by the door, with his head bowed in grief and anger. Opposite him, Tanwen had tucked her knees to her chest and had curled over them with her face pressed into her knees.

Bay rummaged in a drawer labeled "Emergency." Within a few minutes, she had a small scanner in her hands, which she pressed into her forearm. It lit up and gave her some kind of information. "I can get my bio-tech online with this, but I don't understand why the Terr would use a bio-tech specific weapon. That's…" She shook her head. "Why?"

"To demoralize anyone who is a battle veteran, many of whom work at key stations in the Ratterran military forces," Lumien said quietly. "I had heard of this, but I did not imagine the Terr would truly develop it."

Amaya stood and knelt by his side. "Sol."

He glanced up at her with red eyes and shook his head. "My people have betrayed the ideals we are supposed to uphold. I have nothing left."

"You have us…me." She brought his hand to her lips.

Sol caressed her cheek with his other hand. "I know." He leaned in and pressed his forehead against hers. "Your presence, this bond between us, it's holding me together. I know it's hard on you, feeling what I feel. I…can tell you're pulling back, but I understand."

Amaya kissed the corner of his mouth, and then she drew him into a close, fierce hug. "I need you, too. I'm only trying to keep it together. To be the Rayatana. To be fair."

His arms tightened around her, and he rocked her gently back and forth.

Amaya knew they didn't have long, so she tried to memorize this moment, hold him as close as she could, but a boom shook the building.

She gripped Sol even harder, before letting go. "We need to get back out there, help who we can. I'm sure the battle isn't over yet."

Tanwen's hair hung limp around her face, but

she stood slowly. "The block Narra placed on me is beginning to wear off, but I can…handle the swell of emotions now."

"Allow me to help." Bay knelt next to Tanwen and ran the device over Tanwen's bio-tech implant. She pressed a few buttons and hummed. "Yes, I can get this running. Give me a moment."

"We need to check our weapons before we go anywhere. Make sure we're prepared." Narra began checking each of her weapons methodically.

Lumien typed something else on his console, and then he swiveled in his chair to address the room. "We were betrayed from within. That is the only explanation for no one to be at their stations in this room. The way the system works, Cheleth would have alerted anyone connected to the planet. Birk Glowfire took a break, during the testing, leaving it in my mom's hands, and I haven't seen him since it began. We don't know who else has survived the attack, but a large group of witnesses in the arena were ushered out by the majority of Vidarr's team, so I have hope they made it to safety before the Terrs attacked."

Narra paced around the room and stopped in front of Bay. "Your father, Amaya's mother, Captain Prya, and Pilot Geral are most likely safe on their ship." She took the device from Bay's hands. "This scanner shows the repair work you've done on Tanwen and yourself. Your bio-tech is operational, but it could get hit again. If the situation were ideal, I wouldn't take either one of you out there, but as it is, I need at least one of you."

Bay made a fist and pressed it to her shoulder. "I am part of the Rayatana's honor guard, an ally of the Word."

"Someone should stay behind and protect this control room," Amaya said. Plus, it would give Bay a chance to stay safe.

Bay pursed her lips. "I have to guard your back, Amaya. I promised you that."

Lumien slumped back in his chair. "The defense net is up, but I can't communicate with the array, so we can't see what's going on out there."

Amaya leaned over his console, even if she didn't recognize most of the tech. She needed a moment to think.

Tanwen motioned with one hand. "I am capable of fighting. Now that I know my bio-tech could go out, I can fight against my symptoms for a short period of time. One of us needs to stay here and guard Lumien and this room. Please, Bay, allow me to fight this time, and I will allow you to take the next skirmish."

Amazement and shock worked together in Amaya so that a hysterical snort of laughter came out before she could stop it. "Skirmish? I think having bombs dropped on the planet means this is more than a skirmish."

Tanwen pressed her lips together.

"I think Tanwen is just trying to put me at ease," Bay said. She nodded to Tanwen. "Your powers are stronger than mine. This time, I will stay behind. Next time, I fight beside Amaya."

Narra handed Bay the arm cannon she'd taken from one of the Terr attackers. "You might need this more than me. And know this, if you help Lumien get the array up and running, you'll be fighting with Amaya from here." She gave Lumien a sideways glance. "Lumien, I'll send the first Chelethian team I find your way. Keep your communicator on. When they get here, Bay, you can team up with one of them and come to the spaceport. I think the fighting will be hardest there, as different factions and whoever betrayed us tries to get off planet, if they haven't already."

"If we can, we'll stop them," Sol said.

Narra gave him a once-over. "For a Terr Royal, you're all right. I didn't expect that, but I trust you."

Sol dipped his head in acknowledgment.

Amaya appreciated Narra's words. She knew Sol needed to hear them, and it helped to know Narra wouldn't do anything foolish to undermine his ability to fight. Now that they were all ready, she stepped toward the door, intending to go first.

"Wait." Narra stopped her. "I know you're the

Rayatana. I don't doubt it after what I've seen, but I know this planet. Cheleth is my home. I know the best ways between here and the spaceport. I need you to follow my lead, at least until we get there."

Amaya glanced at Tanwen and Sol, and they curtly agreed. They were all worse for the wear — torn clothes, bruised, their eyes weary — but they each held a core of determination inside them, a desire to save Cheleth and the people they loved.

Amaya stepped aside and allowed Narra to take the lead. "I will listen."

Narra faced the door. "Open it."

ON THE STREETS

Sol opened the door with one hand. In his other hand, he held a grenjen.

The quiet hallway was unnerving. The bodies of the Terr they had killed lay in heaps. Amaya tried to turn away from the destruction but couldn't. They had done this with their combined power, and power had a price.

Tanwen and Sol left the room, Amaya followed them, and Narra took up the rear. They walked cautiously down the hallway and into the main library, pausing at each corner.

No hint of sound inside the building alerted them to anyone's presence. Distant booms of weapons hit the net-shield high above in the atmosphere.

Narra stopped and took note of the surrounding library. "We'll take the back exit." She led them through a series of stacks of books, down a set of stairs, and then up another set to a wide door that reminded Amaya of an industrial drop-off area.

Narra stopped them again. "We're going to follow alongside the path, cut right through a group of buildings, and take a back alley to the spaceport." She paused a beat before kicking open the door, with a grenjen in one hand and an arm cannon on the other.

The sound of weapons' fire came closer.

Narra took a step outside, motioned to them, and took off running. Amaya, Sol, and Tanwen ran in a single-file line behind her. They traversed alongside the path, but not on it, ducking through the brush, and weaving into a small stand of ornamental trees. Next to them on the left, a wide expanse of gardens offered no protection from the attackers and no visual evidence of the current struggle.

Narra turned to the right and cut through two low buildings. Amaya stayed close to her and had to jump to the side when Narra halted.

A Terr soldier had turned down their street, followed by three or four more of them. The first soldier raised his weapon to fire.

Amaya pulled on her power, which responded quickly, but not before Narra took the first soldier down.

When the other soldiers brought up their weapons, Amaya blasted them with two streams of warm, gold energy. Her intent, to protect her friends, shone through the color.

Narra touched her sleeve. "They're down. Let's go back and take a different street."

"Nice work, Amaya," Tanwen said. "You're gaining control of it quickly."

Sol's affirmation came through the Zoe Bond.

Smiling slightly, Amaya motioned for Narra to continue, who turned right away. She followed Narra, with Sol and Tanwen next to her.

To the left, a small group of Terr soldiers walked away from them, farther down the street. To the right, another group of Terr soldiers had several Chelethians cornered against the front of a building.

Amaya turned in that direction, but Narra whispered, "No, we need to get to our objective."

Amaya gritted her teeth in frustration. She needed to get to them. The muscles around her rib cage tightened with the need to move, to do something to change the horror happening around them.

Narra waited for a moment more and waved her hand forward. "Run."

They crossed the intersection in a rush. On the other side, a shout from one of the Terr soldiers reached Amaya, and she started to turn.

"No, let me handle this," Tanwen said.

Amaya pivoted to stop her, but Tanwen was

already ready. Her hands glowed two different colors, and her eyes and skin brightened as more power filled her. Throwing one arm forward, she sent a stream of purple tinged power toward the attackers.

Amaya didn't wait to see the outcome. She chased after Narra with Sol beside her.

When they ducked into an alleyway behind the main market street, they startled a group of Chelethian children hiding behind a large orange crate oozing with leftover food and some kind of insect, like a dumpster on Earth.

One of the children cried out, but Narra put up her weapons. "It's all right. Follow us."

The child pointed at Sol, "But he's one of them…"

"He isn't one of those who attack us," Narra explained. "I know a place where you can stay safe. It's a bit farther down."

They walked now, staying with the four children, who held hands and gave Sol fear-filled glances. Amaya wished she could soothe them, but they didn't have time, and she didn't know how.

Narra looked to be searching for something, and finally, she said, "Ah, the fish market." She fished out a set of keys and opened the door to the back of a market. The funky smell of sea life from a different planet stunk up the air, in much the same way it would on Earth.

"You'll be safe here, children. It stinks too much for anyone to search it." Narra gave a forced chuckle.

One of the children barked out a hysterical laugh, while the rest stared around their surroundings warily.

Amaya stood guard while the children hid behind a set of vats meant to keep live specimens. "Good plan."

Narra locked the door behind them when they left, and they continued down the alleyway. Amaya stayed close at Narra's heels, with Sol beside her again. A silence filled with caution and dread surrounded their light footfalls.

Tanwen still hadn't rejoined them, and Amaya hoped she was all right. She had almost wanted to ask Narra if they could wait for Tanwen, but after their errand with the children, she wasn't sure if Tanwen had fallen behind them somewhere, or if she had passed them.

They reached the edge of the alleyway, closest to the inner side of the spaceport.

Narra ducked behind a bin filled with old cargo carriers, and Amaya followed suit.

Sol knelt behind her.

Narra peeked out from their hiding place, crouched down again, and reported. "Five Terr units have one of the Ratterran ships surrounded. The other is gone. Your ship is also surrounded, but it looks as though they can't get inside. That Terr woman, Belryus, is beating up Rayal while two others hold him down. Not sure if she wants information or if she is just that twisted."

"She's that twisted," Sol said.

The responsibility for her people weighed on Amaya and spurred her forward a half-step, but Narra put a hand on her arm. "We can't help him if we don't have a plan."

Amaya sighed; Narra was right. She crouched back down, squatting on her heels, ready to move when they could.

"There are several groups of Chelethian Security Forces and our military on the ground, as if they've surrendered. I haven't received a response from the Council Leaders." Narra tapped her communicator again. It lit up orange, which made her grimace. "That means they're unable to answer."

Amaya stared at a line of insects marching up and down the nearest wall of the alleyway. It made her think of how the way Terr treated others around them, as following orders from one central unit like insects in a hive. Did their Charm have that effect, and what would happen if… "What if we create a large enough distraction to get them away from the ships? Will that help at all? Is there any way the three of us can take on the number of Terr out there?"

"They have…they have a weakness," Sol said. "My people rely on their power to do their work for them." He cocked his head toward Narra. "How many of the Terr Protectorate are using their powers?"

Narra peeked over the edge of their hiding place again. When she crouched down, she kept her eyes on Sol. "None of them." She flicked open a device on her utility belt. A hiss escaped her lips. "They are using the power dampeners and have created a field as wide as the spaceport. How is that possible? I don't know, but if we break the field, we could set our forces free, help Rayal, and turn this around."

"Now that sounds like a plan," Amaya said. "How do we execute it?"

"You don't," a voice behind them said.

DAMPENING WEIGHT

As her power welled up, a heavy weight came down on Amaya, and her powered diminished to nothing. A vise grip of pain encircled her head, and she fell to the ground. She blinked and blinked, but it was hard to keep her eyelids open against the light of the sky. Next to her, Narra lay on the ground, with her hands cuffed behind her back. Sol's pain and confusion pounded through the Zoe Bond. She tried to send back assurance, an assurance she didn't feel, but the weight pressed down on her even more. She closed her eyes, still awake, fighting the heaviness, the hollowness, the missing piece where her power should be. Still, deeper, she felt the thread of the Zoe Bond, Sol's heartbeat, his trust and dedication to her. It kept her awake, even though she could sense him slipping away.

She could not allow him to die.

"Take them to Belryus. She'll want something special for these two, especially him." A deep voice in a Terr accent gave direction to the others. One of the attackers picked up Sol. Another Terr soldier grabbed Amaya by an arm and a leg and threw her over wide shoulders in a fireman's carry. Amaya pretended to be unconscious by relaxing her muscles so she would be as limp as a rag doll. She watched her surroundings through half-closed eyelids.

The soldiers carried them into the spaceport hangar, in the direction of Belryus, who continued to hit Rayal with gloved fists.

The weight of the power dampener and her own despair dragged at Amaya's consciousness. What can I do? How can I defeat Belryus? Given the way her companions were unconscious or drifting in and out, it didn't seem as though the dampener net was the same kind as the Chelethian Security Team used. What have they done to us? How can I fight it?

Before she could formulate an idea, the soldier dumped her on the hard surface of the spaceport hanger. A kick to her stomach left her gasping. Tears streamed from her eyes.

Belryus bent forward and sneered into Amaya's face. "Well, well, this is the famed Rayatana, the savior of The Great Galaxy, the bringer of peace for all tuigseach throughout the known universe."

The fools hadn't cuffed her, and Amaya shot out a hand and punched Belryus in the throat.

Belryus fell back a step. She clutched her throat, coughing. When she spoke, it came out in a rasp.

"You…you reglaf!"

Amaya's memory-cube download hadn't included swear words, but she was pretty sure "reglaf" didn't mean anything good. She tried to shove herself to her feet, but her arms gave out.

"Cuff her," Belryus shouted.

Soldiers surrounded Amaya. Seconds later, she was cuffed with her hands behind her. The metal pinched her wrists. As soon as they were finished, they drew back, and Belryus took a running kick at her face.

Amaya twisted and rolled, so that Belryus's kick impacted the back of her shoulder. She kept moving, knowing Belryus wouldn't be satisfied with a near miss.

"Get her on her knees and hold her there," Belryus ordered.

They grabbed Amaya, dragging her onto her knees until she knelt in front of Belryus, who sneered, even with a hand at her throat. Her eyes crackled with power.

The weight of the power dampeners pressed into Amaya's skull.

Belryus bombarded Amaya with power, and the bright light hit Amaya hard in the eyes, but she didn't close them. It hurt, but at the same time, the dampeners somehow lifted off her. Her body regained strength as the power poured into her, not against her.

When Belryus stopped, Amaya smirked.

"What is this?" Belryus shrieked. "This is impossible."

"Is it?"

The last of the dampener's hold broke away.

Amaya flexed her fingers behind her back and surged her power toward her hands.

The cuffs melted off.

On her feet, she commanded her power to blaze bright from her eyes. "Let my people and the people of Cheleth go."

Belryus stepped back, shielding her eyes. "Impossible."

"I don't think you know the meaning of that word in any language."

Sol's amazement and pride flowed into her and gave her even more strength. Her power responded to his, and she expanded her bubble of shield to include him, Narra, and Rayal.

"Loyal Terrs, open fire on this woman," Belryus shouted.

Weapons opened fire around them.

Amaya raised her hands and directed her power to create a shield. The weapons' fire struck the shield of light around her but didn't penetrate. Warmth spread through Amaya, and she recognized the feeling: confidence. I can do this.

With that thought in mind, she stepped toward Belryus while channeling more power into her shield.

Belryus fell back. Her mouth gaped open, and her eyes widened. She shouted something Amaya couldn't hear.

The barrage of weapons continued.

Amaya kept her shield up and stepped closer to Belryus.

Belryus pivoted and sprinted away, waving and shouting at her soldiers, who formed a half-circle behind her as they headed to their ship. Four of the Terr soldiers grabbed an unconscious figure off the ground and started hauling their burden toward the ship.

Amaya dashed toward the Terr ship, not wanting to allow them to take anyone. When she recognized her mom, she screamed and sent a raw bludgeon of power through her shield at the Terrs. It hit one of them in the legs, and the solider fell, dropping her mom on the ground.

Amaya struck another Terr with power, but this one twisted on the way down. When he rolled, he brought up his weapon. Even though her shield deflected the weapon, her mom was still vulnerable. She raced toward the Terr and her mom, who was still unconscious on the ground.

Realizing her intent, the Terr turned his weapon on her mom, pointing it at her head.

"No!" Amaya dropped her shields and sent an uncontrolled blast of power into the Terr.

He flew backward across the spaceport and smacked into a ship.

A streak from one of the Terr's weapons ripped through her shoulder with a hard punch of pain, and Amaya went down onto one knee. She refocused on her shield until it bubbled up around her and encompassed her mom as well.

The remaining Terr fired on her while backing up into their ship.

Amaya wanted to stop them, but she was losing blood, even as she clamped a hand over her shoulder, pressing painfully onto the wound.

The Terr ship's engines rumbled.

Several Chelethians lay in the danger zone too close to the ship. The take-off blast could kill them. No longer attacked by weapons' fire, Amaya forced all her energy into her shield and expanded it to cover those by the Terr ship. Dots of darkness appeared on the edge of her vision.

With fiery thunder, the Terr ship took off, and waves of heat rushed over her shield. Amaya collapsed before she could see if her shield had held long enough.

FACTIONS

A thick pungent odor brought Amaya awake with a hard sneeze. "What is that smell?"

"Wake-weed," Narra said matter-of-factually, waving a foul-smelling, purple herb in front of Amaya's face.

Amaya squeezed her nose shut. "Okay. I'm awake."

"It took us longer than I thought it would to wake you, so I wanted to make sure." Narra put the weed inside a capsule and stuck it in one of the pouches on her belt. She held out her hand.

Amaya took her hand, and Narra helped her into a good sitting position.

Amaya glanced around the spaceport. A flurry of med-techs wearing signature green and white clothes had set up a make-shift triage center. Tuigseach from all over The Great Galaxy huddled around each other and gave one another aid. "Where is my crew?

Are they all right?"

Narra opened her palms and waved one hand to indicate an area farther in the spaceport. "The Power Dampeners are down. After your power surge, they faltered long enough for some of our people to shut them off manually. Tanwen saw to your injury. She took out that squad we left her against, and then she came here in time to stabilize you. She also said that since you have begun to understand your power, you can work on your wounds, but you need to rest longer before you try it." Narra glanced around. "The Terr Protectorate retreated from the system, but the Neutral Zone Treaty Alliance is no longer neutral. There will be a meeting here and a meeting on the Bannard Orbiting Station, the home of the Neutral Zone Treaty Alliance."

"Before we get to that, can you tell me if my team is okay? Did my mom make it?"

"Yes, you saved them, and the rest of us. Your mother and the others are resting in the ship, and you will join them soon, but I have been tasked with asking you this—" Narra paused and gave Amaya a level gaze. Her brown eyes deepened into dark pools, a different power than Amaya had. "Will you join with us to defeat the Terr and bring peace once more to The Great Galaxy?"

Amaya wanted to immediately say yes, but something held her frozen. This could be one of her choices Tanwen had mentioned, and she had to get it right.

The moment stretched out. The air felt hot and heavy with the weight of expectations. The people of Cheleth, and many others, would be depending on her, but according to the prophecy she was supposed to save the whole Great Galaxy, not just one planet or one group.

"What do you mean by 'defeat' them? And what will you do to sustain peace? I would need to know more before I agree," Amaya said and lifted her hands. "I need to know I am on a path of long-term peace, not vengeance. This power could be ill-used otherwise."

Narra nodded, her smile growing. "Citra said you would be wise enough to ask." She sighed. "I would rather bring a firm answer back to my people, but Citra noticed something when she connected to Cheleth. There is rot in the roots, where Birk was connected. She will stay here to ensure he cannot do more damage." Narra shaded her eyes and glanced behind them.

Amaya twisted to see what Narra saw. The great tree of Cheleth was visible through the buildings. Some of it was broken, burned, and fractured from the rest. "Will it heal?"

"I think so. While I cannot speak for Cheleth or my people, I thank you, Amaya, and know this: if you need me, I will answer, regardless of what my people do. I am now and forever a Raya." She made a fist with her hand, laid it over her heart, her head, and then she held it out to Amaya.

"I am honored." Amaya took the stout hand in her own and gave it a firm grip.

DIRECTION

While Narra took her decision and her questions back to the Chelethian Council, Amaya surveyed the spaceport and did not feel triumphant. Despite the victory over the Terr Protectorate's incursion forces, Chelethians of all tuigseach races lay dead or wounded around the spaceport. The Med-techs worked at a frantic pace. She wanted to help, but she swayed on her feet.

She took a long turn, pivoting on her feet to see the full damage. There, Tanwen stood over a child. Her hands were lit up in a healing glow. In another direction, Citra towered above a group of Chelethians, seemingly arguing with her arms raised. Lumien, with his arms crossed, glared at Birk Glowfire, who appeared to be defying Citra more than anyone. Narra headed toward them.

Amaya didn't want to be drawn into their argument. She needed to check on her team. Sol was anxious about something, but not in pain or anger. She trudged to the ship. Every muscle of her body ached with exhaustion.

When she was halfway there, Sol dashed out and held out his arms to her.

She fell into his embrace, enjoying the press of his shoulder against her cheek, the soft sensation of his breath in her hair, and the way his hands pressed into her back. She squeezed him tight, and then she released him enough to tilt her head up at him.

"Narra said she'd take care of you, but you feel so tired through our bond. I was worried." Sol tightened his grip on her.

"I'm worn out. Nothing that rest won't fix." Amaya gave him another squeeze. "Is my mom okay?"

His mouth drew down, and his shoulders slumped. "Roxana is…physically weakened by all that has happened, and she is fearful of going anywhere; on the ship and outside of it."

Amaya could imagine her mother being stubborn but had a hard time picturing her afraid. "She trained me for so much, but she…isn't ready for all this."

He nodded and relaxed his embrace. "She thinks you can stay here and lead the Neutral Zone Alliance into the war zone through words and leadership."

Amaya shook her head. "That's not going to happen."

He nodded his head toward Citra and the other Chelethians. "They didn't ask you?"

"They did. There's something off. I asked Narra what they meant by 'defeat' the Terr and what their idea of peace looked like. She's relaying my questions to them. I feel like there's something I'm missing, a piece I don't understand. And it has something to do with Citra and the message Chol left us. I should be over there, but I wanted to check on my crew first."

"The crew, your mom, or me?" He raised his eyebrows and drew her closer to him. His gaze focused on her lips.

She tilted her head up and quirked one eyebrow. "All of the above, but I also wanted to hold you."

His gaze softened, and he tugged her a little closer, leaned down, and then paused. "Amaya?"

Tingling heat coursed through her. She reached up, traced the curve of his jaw until she could tangle her fingertips in his soft wave of hair. She touched her lips to his, and he deepened their kiss.

A cough interrupted them.

They drew apart.

Bay rolled her eyes. "In the middle of a battlefield? Really? Lip-locking?"

Amaya rubbed the back of her neck. "We had some unfinished business. And yes, making sure the person you love knows it, well, it's worth it." Amaya's cheeks burned, and she stepped back. Had she just said love? She hadn't meant to say that, not yet.

Sol rubbed the top of her shoulder with his thumb. Joy ran through their Zoe Bond, and Amaya basked in it like the warmth of a sun.

Bay put up her hands in surrender. "Please, get serious. The Chelethians are arguing, your mom wants to join one of the Ratterran ships, and my dad thinks we need to stay here and lead the former-Neutral Zone Treaty Alliance against the Terr Protectorate. Unless I'm missing something, your love fest isn't going to create peace for The Great Galaxy."

Amaya placed one hand on the pendant of her necklace. "I have to make a choice. A big one. The right one."

Lumien dashed across the spaceport and interrupted their conversation by holding up a hand. "Please. My mom needs you over there. Birk is misleading the Chelethians, and I am…angry at him, angrier than I've ever felt." His glow seared brighter.

Bay shifted her weight toward him, then away, her hands fluttering up, then back to her hips. "Lumien, we can help." She directed her gaze to Amaya. "Right?"

"Yes. We'll help Citra." She left the comfort of Sol's arm around her shoulder and trekked across the spaceport toward Citra and Birk Glowfire. The others fell in beside her.

She heard the argument before they were even close.

Birk raised his staff above his head, and shouted, "I am the Branch of Cheleth, and I will so remain!" He brought the staff down on the solid surface of the spaceport, but it merely thumped against the ground. The staff had changed, from a living branch with fresh leaves to a dead branch with no leaves and dry bark.

Citra placed one hand around Birk's staff and held it in place as Birk attempted to wrest it away from her. Compared to her, he looked like a blustering storm breaking on a solid rock. Citra placed one of her glowing hands on Birk's shoulder. "Cheleth has rejected you because you betrayed us. I am the new branch."

Birk placed his hand against his mouth and stepped back. "I…thought I could save us. It is why I allowed the Terr Protectorate to break free of the prison. I thought they would leave us alone if we gave them this girl claiming to be the Rayatana."

Citra's glow intensified. "Claiming?"

"I understand now. She is." Birk bowed from his waist toward Amaya. "You have my most humble respect and allegiance." He spoke these words with his gaze on the floor.

Amaya rubbed her ear and stepped back. She clenched her stomach. She didn't think he was telling the truth, and wouldn't trust him. She inched closer to Citra.

"Citra? What is your need and Cheleth's need at this time? As the Rayatana, I am tasked with creating peace for the whole of The Great Galaxy. I have also been tasked with finding the Rayatana Candidates from Earth who were taken by the Terr Protectorate. I need to find them. I think they may be the key to fulfilling my greater destiny."

"She has no right to speak for Cheleth!" Birk sprang forward with a sharp blade in his hand. He plunged it at Citra.

Amaya tried to step between them, but Citra's glow changed colors rapidly, and tendrils of roots burst up from the soil, creating a shield between them and Birk.

As Birk shouted in frustration, roots wove around his arms and legs, imprisoning him, but not connecting to him the way they had during the trial. "No! I am the Branch of Cheleth. Please, Cheleth, I seek to protect you." A root wound its way around Birk's mouth and his speech was muffled, but his nose was free for breathing.

Amaya clenched her hands together. "What will happen to him?"

When Citra spoke this time, her voice was joined by the rustling of leaves from the great tree behind them, echoing and magnifying her words. "I am Cheleth, speaking to you through Citra, the Branch of Cheleth and Cheleth's voice. Since the birth of my planet, I have only joined once before with a Glower, and now, because I have again, my power is magnified. Allies, I call to you to stand with me to protect the Neutral Zone Alliance from any warring parties. We will not go on offense but create a strong set of branches around the Neutral Zone to save those who do not yearn for war and seek power in their roots. This one, Birk, has lost his way, and we will keep him in a safe place until he is ready to see what it truly means to protect the people of his planet and the Neutral Zone."

The rest of the Chelethians who had circled Citra backed away at the words of Cheleth pouring through Citra. Those who had sided with Birk retreated from the rest of the crowd.

Narra spoke into her wrist-com, "Chelethian Security Team Five, we need you to take care of Birk Glowfire and his accomplices." She walked over to Birk's supporters and spoke to them, as Chelethian Security Team Five surrounded them.

The rest of the crowd dispersed and Citra, her arms attached to the roots around her by tiny rootlets, turned to Amaya. "Amaya Iris Benson, the Rayatana, you've been tasked with peace, not war. It is well for you to remember this. I give you leave to find your kind, the children of three worlds, the children who do not claim one heritage over another. You will be a nexus for peace. Go, and take my son with you. He has the map to the Rayatana Candidates, though he does not know it yet. And you will need the other Terr prince, the one you despise. He will guide you."

Amaya's gut tightened. She knew exactly who Citra-Cheleth was talking about. "How do you know about Chol?"

Citra held out her arms. Branches and roots lifted her up off the ground. "My roots encircle the entire planet. My people inhabit the star ways of The Great Galaxy. We worship the Triple One, and we do what we were seeded to do. A task like yours, but over many more years."

"There is more than one Cheleth?"

Amusement rippled through Citra and through the great tree's leaves. "No, child. Cheleth is my name as Amaya is yours. But my people's time is coming to an end, and our name needs not to be remembered."

Citra sighed as the rootlets released her, and the roots sank to the ground under her feet. She held out her arms to Lumien, and he hugged her. "Mom."

Amaya stepped away to give them their privacy and to consider what she had learned. While Cheleth's power and reach was as frightening as it was awe-inspiring, it had affirmed her choice, and she would take that as a commendation.

MATTERS OF THE HEART

Entering Rayatana Prime, the spaceship disguised as an Earth movie theater, Amaya breathed in the smell of popcorn and licorice, and breathed out some of her tension. The movie posters in the lobby were comforting, lit up by the lights in the hallway and surrounded by gold frames. The red carpet was scuffed, but no one stood in the lobby. Amaya stood still for a moment and took it all in. The reds and golds, the completely raided snack stand, the hallway leading to the two theaters, and she imagined, just for a moment, she was back on Earth before this all began. She remembered her unhappiness over the move to a small town away from her friends in California, friends who had never returned her texts, her contentment at finding new friends who seemed so innocent of her mom's plans, and her sense of needing to hide out, of not having a purpose. And now, she had new friends and a new purpose, but she still had to deal with her mom.

The thought brought her sharply back to reality,

and she marched over to the command center, which had once been a ticket stand. She jabbed the intercom button. "All hands to Theater One. We need to have a meeting."

As she walked across the lobby area and entered the hallway, Sol wrapped an arm around her shoulder. Amaya paused at the entryway of the theater. She smoothed down her Trial shirt, which didn't make it look more presentable, given the dirt, stains, and wrinkles on it after a day of battle. "You go first."

Sol kissed her forehead.

A loud sigh from behind them broke the moment.

Amaya pivoted to face Bay who had her arms crossed. "Lip-locking again? You called the meeting, remember?"

Amaya smirked. "Well, that means I get to start it when I'm ready."

Bay rolled her eyes and walked past them into Theater One.

Sol saluted her with a wink and walked into the theater behind Bay.

Amaya entered Theater One and climbed onto the small stage in front of the tall screen. She paced back and forth until everyone entered the room, noting where each of them sat and whom they sat with.

Rayal, his red Ratterran jacket snug on his shoulders, but unbuttoned at the front, showing his injuries had healed had a seat in the front row, next to Bay, who still wore her trial uniform as Amaya did. He leaned over to speak quietly to Bay, and Bay shook her head in response.

Sol sat in a seat in the same row as Bay and Rayal, but he sat two seats down from them, center to the stage. He watched Amaya as she paced, fully attentive. She couldn't get distracted by him, so she gazed beyond him to the doorway. Her mom, Prya, and Geral all entered together. Prya and Geral walked with her mom who held her arms crossed her waist. They took seats in the second row behind Sol. Amaya's mom gave her a pleading look, with eyes wide and wet with tears.

Amaya ran a hand over her neck, and then dropped it to her side. She didn't want to appear nervous or uncomfortable. She straightened her shoulders just as Tanwen and Lumien appeared in the doorway together. Tanwen wore her trial clothes, and they had blood all over them, presumably from injuries she'd been helping to heal. Lumien wore his technician clothes from the trial, but in addition to his tool belt he also wore a bandolier style weapon's belt over his shoulder and a small pack.

"We heard you called a meeting," Tanwen said, as she took a seat in the third row. "Bay notified us since we were still outside tending to Chelethian affairs."

Amaya nodded to Bay. "Thank you."

Bay shrugged and held out one hand and rolled it, as if to say, "on with it."

Amaya took the center of the stage. "I called this meeting for two reasons. To give a short explanation and to give direction."

Amaya's mom leaned forward. "Who has advised you in this direction?"

Amaya swallowed back a sigh. "I will explain events as I see them, first. Then I'll give direction. It will be up to you if you decided to follow me. But know this, my path is set."

She gathered her courage and began. "From what I understand, my grandparents were one of many tuigseach, or as Earthers might call them, intelligent alien beings, who sought refuge on Earth from war in The Great Galaxy. For generations, these tuigseach have intermarried and lived on Earth. Many Rayatana Candidates have been born on Earth. I was protected by my mother, and she trained me to fight, survive, and make decisions. For that, I am thankful." She nodded to her mom.

Her mom sat up straight and lifted her chin.

That moment wasn't going to last. Amaya continued. "But in this protection, I did not know anything about my heritage, or my people. The Rayatana Candidates are my people. I know those who believe in the prophecies about the Rayatana are called the Raya, but I believe this is the name for my people as well, the children of multiple worlds. We are the Raya. And I need them to complete the task to bring peace to The Great Galaxy."

Her mom's lips tightened into a thin line.

Amaya glanced at Sol, then Bay, then Tanwen, and Lumien. Sol put his fist to his heart. Bay nodded. Tanwen gazed down at her lap, and Lumien leaned forward.

"Cheleth has chosen Citra as a Branch, has forgiven us for our trespasses here, and has given me a commendation to pursue the Raya, to find them, and to complete my task. Lumien, Citra's son, will help us." She waved her hand to him.

He stood.

The others turned to see him before turning back to her.

Lumien resumed his seat.

Amaya tilted her head downward. After a moment, she faced the room again. "But there is something more difficult that Cheleth recommended: Chol as our guide."

Rayal stood and smacked a fist against his leg. "No. We cannot allow that scum on board this ship. This whole plan, to go chasing after a group of Raya, is untenable at best, but with Chol, it is doomed to fail from the start. We can do more good here, with the Neutral Zone Alliance."

Amaya held up a hand. "Which has been tasked with protecting the borders of Neutral Zone Worlds, not with an attack on the Terr Protectorate. Cheleth has decided this."

Rayal stepped back. "I will speak with Citra. My people need to deal with the threat of the Terr Protectorate, or we will never have peace."

Amaya flared her power as a warning, which forced him to sit down in his seat. "You are one of my Honor Guard, or have you forgotten?"

Rayal stared at his feet. "No, but the Rayatana would give her people a choice."

"True. You each have a choice. You can join me in my task, or you can stay on Cheleth. I ask you to come with me, to deal with Chol if we must, and to rescue the Raya. Will you?"

Bay stood and saluted. "I will, Rayatana."

Rayal grabbed her arm. "Bay?"

Bay pulled away from him. "I will go with Amaya. She needs my help, and I believe she will lead us to peace, although the path there may be a struggle."

Rayal stood and stared at his daughter. His chest heaved as he took gasping breaths. Finally, he shook his head. "So, the time has come, then, for us to part paths."

Bay held out her hand. "It doesn't have to."

Rayal shook his head. "Our people need me."

Bay raised her hands and waved them at the room. "Yes, OUR people do. All of our people from The Great Galaxy. Not just one people. I thought you believed in the Rayatana and would do anything for her if the true Rayatana came. Well, she's here, and you know it."

Rayal glanced at Amaya. "I believe you are the Rayatana, Amaya, but my people do need me, the Ratterran people need me. I need to speak with our leadership, share what I have learned here."

"If you change your mind, you can rejoin us at any time, Rayal. I would be honored to have you, and any of the Ratterran people with us." Amaya gave him a short salute, with her head only bowed partway.

Rayal put his fist to his chest and bowed at the waist. "Thank you, Rayatana." He straightened. "Are you sure about needing Chol?"

Amaya crossed her arms. "Cheleth told me we would need him."

Rayal ran a hand over his chin. "I will alert my people to change their orders, to only capture and not kill him on sight."

Shock hit her in the gut and Amaya's power flared again. "That wasn't your order to give."

Rayal bowed his head. "I understand, Rayatana."

"You will stay in communication with me about

decisions like this from here forward, and if you will not serve in my Honor Guard, you will send five of your best to take your place."

Rayal's shoulders shifted back and he lifted his chin. "They will be honored to serve you."

As Amaya has suspected, Rayal responded to both a threat and a compliment. Implying only five of his best could fill his shoes gave him a compliment and he couldn't seem to refuse those.

She pivoted to the rest of the theater. "Does anyone else have concerns?"

Sol walked over to stand next to Bay. "I would be proud to call Bay my ally, and you know I will follow you wherever you go, Amaya."

Amaya smiled briefly, and then she glanced at her mom, whose lips seemed permanently pressed into a hard line.

Her mom pressed her hands together. "I do not believe this is the right path, Amaya. I have come to have a new appreciation for the power you hold, but I do not believe chasing down failed candidates is the right way to be the Rayatana."

Amaya clenched her hands into fists, then she slowly released them. "I know that it is, despite what you believe. You can remain on this ship, or you can choose to stay on Cheleth."

"Or she can come with me." Rayal stepped

forward. "My people rarely use their power noticeably, so she would be comfortable there."

Amaya's mom glanced at him. "Thank you, Rayal. I would like Amaya to listen to reason, but since she will not" — she shook her head at Amaya curtly — "I will stay here on Cheleth, or with you people."

Amaya's chest felt as though it had taken on the weight of a star ship. "Mom."

Her mom's face lit up with a tight grin of triumph. "You've come to your senses, then?"

Amaya crossed her arms in front of her chest again. "No. You can stay here. I will miss you, but I know you'll be safe."

Lumien stood and joined Amaya's mom. "I can ensure you have a place to stay if you wish to stay planet-side." He glanced back at Amaya. "Don't leave without me."

"We won't."

Amaya's mom glanced at Lumien. "You don't need to help me. I can manage on my own." She headed for the door, leaving Lumien standing there, bewildered.

Rayal nodded to Amaya. "I'll watch over her."

"Thank you."

Throat tight and chest heavy, Amaya watched her mom and Rayal the theater. She didn't want her mom to leave like this, but she didn't know what else she could do. She knew her mission, and she knew her mom wasn't going to accept it.

When the door swung shut behind her mom, Amaya turned a glassy-eyed gaze on the others.

Prya and Geral walked to the front of the theater and saluted her. "We will come." Prya smiled. "I'm guessing you knew that since I had already named my ship Rayatana Prime."

"Yes." Amaya attempted to smile back, but she cleared her throat instead. "Thank you."

Tanwen came to join the others. "I believe you've made the right choice."

Amaya wiped at her eyes and placed her hand on her pendant. "I hope so."

***

Much later, as the others stocked provisions, Amaya sat down in the front row of Theater One and stared up at the dark screen. It had all started here. From a small theater to a living planet, and now, beyond to rescue the Raya. So much had changed, but she was still the same woman inside. She gazed down at the interlocking ovals on her pendant.

"Three worlds. Three choices," she said to herself. "What does it mean that I've only been to two worlds so far? Have I made the right choices? Will I make the ones leading to peace?"

"Yes," Sol said, from behind her.

She'd known he was there, because of their Bond, but she hadn't realized how close he was. He held a popcorn bucket in his hands.

"I thought you might like some company."

Amaya smiled. If nothing else went right, Sol would have her back. At least she could be sure of that.

BRIEF GLOSSARY
OF TERMS

Note: Some terms have more than one definition

Tuigseach: any intelligent life form or people group, and an important term for understanding the glossary

Arm-cannon: a weapon strapped to the forearm with a heavy strike

Bio-tech: technology interfaced with the biology of the user to overcome a variety of health issues and disabilities. Some bio-tech is considered dangerous and cutting edge

Cheleth: a neutral zone planet, on which this story takes place

Ddraigons: tuigseach who resemble Earth's idea of dragons

Ddraigon Kins: tuigseach formed by Ddraigon and another species

Awak: a stimulating drink, normally served warm, much like coffee or tea

Earthborn: any tuigseach born on Earth

Dampener: technology which dampens the powers of powered individuals

Dryadarians: tuigseach who have plant and humanoid forms

Gifts/Powers: abilities which enable a tuigseach to do things against the laws of Xia

Granchan: a hearty stew made with fruits and vegetables, originated on Verde

Grenjen: a photo weapon

Glowers: tuigseach who love being mysterious

Memory-cube: a device which downloads information into the minds of most tuigseach

Nardels: a native animal of Cheleth, hunted to near-extinction

Photo-medicine: medicine based on light waves and particles

Order of Raya: those who have dedicated their lives to the Rayatana

Rayatana: Child of Three Worlds prophesied to end The Thousand Years' War; or, Friend of the Stars

Ratterrans: tuigseach who broke from the Terrs

Ratterran Alliance: an alliance of nine planets formed by the Ratterran Elite

Reglaf: a Terr insult and curse word, untranslated

Space Defense Force: an Earth-based space defense system

Terrs: tuigseach residing on the planet Terran in the Faran Galaxy

Terr Protectorate: nine planets and a solar system under the protection of the Terr Empire

The Great Galaxy: Earthborn call it The Milky Way Galaxy

The Thousand Years' War: an ongoing conflict between Terrs and Ratterrans

The Triple One: sometimes called the Three-in-One God of the Universe

Trial of Integrity: a series of tests and questions designed to determine the intention and/or guilt of a person who may/may not have committed a crime

Verde: the home planet of the Dryadarian

Wake-weed: The Chelethian version of Smelling Salts

Xiatat: a universal language and money system for trade between tuigseach

Xia: another name for The Great Galaxy; or, a being worshiped by many

ABOUT THE AUTHOR

Tyrean Martinson is a word hunter. She forages for words both sweet and tart in the South Sound of Washington State. An eclectic writer, she writes speculative fiction, contemporary and historical fiction, short scripts, devotions, writing books, song lyrics, and poetry. She has been a fencer (long ago), a kick boxer (for a short minute), and an action-movie fan. She is a life-long book lover, a Christ follower, and walker. Once upon a time, she was a Girl Scout who sang too loudly, and now she's a pod caster and praise team member. Since childhood, her imagination has been swept away by fairy tales, science fiction, tales of overcoming the odds, and redemption arcs.

To find Tyrean or her books, visit her Link Tree: **linktr.ee/Tyrean**

ACKNOWLEDGEMENTS

Many thanks to my family, especially my husband and my daughters; my father-in-law who is "amazed by imagination" and my parents who are excited to read anything I write; to my friends, encouragers, Bible study sisters, and both in-person and online writing buddies; and to my exquisite editor Chrys Fey, and my amazing cover artist Carrie Butler.

Next, I want to give a huge shout-out to all of the amazing people who helped me launch Liftoff in 2020, many of whom volunteered to help with ARCs and book party celebrations for Nexus this year! These peeps are amazing and kind, and not listed in order of their awesomeness or the alphabet, so I am hoping I haven't forgotten anyone: Patricia Josephine, Tara Tyler, L. Diane Wolfe, Alex J. Cavanaugh, Susan M. Gourley, Jacqui Murray, Jemi Fraser, Chrys Fey (again!), Diane M Burton, Amanda Tillet, Lynda R. Young, Milo James Fowler, Cathrina Constantine, Natalie Aguirre, Jessica Fred Martinson Roberts, Lynn Glover, MJ Fifield, Erika Beebe, C. Lee McKenzie, Toi Thomas, Shana Dow, Sherry Ellis, Carol Riggs, Tonja Drecker, Cindy Vincent, EC Murray, Julia Larson, Kathy Guy, Beth Camp, Mary Lanni, to all of the Insecure Writer's Support Group, to all the retweets by my Twitter friends, and shout-outs by Instagram friends, to Jackie Casella and the Creative Colloquy team for giving me a chance to give readings at online open mic events, and to Larry Fowler of the Greater Gig Harbor Literary Society for giving me and fellow writers an opportunity to share and sign books at business and events. Many, many thanks to all of you. Without you, this book would not be finished.

Due to a recent post by someone in the Instagram community, I also want to give a shout-out to some of my teachers who encouraged me to write and to dream: to my third grade teacher Mrs. Bolognesi, for the assignment that spurred my first speculative fiction story and for giving me a chance to grow; to my fifth grade teacher Mr. Morrison, for reminding me that I needed to keep my feet on the ground as well as in books; to my sixth grade teacher Mrs. O'Connell for telling me for the first time that I could be an author and for encouraging me to write the "Pencil Who Ran Away from School" and "The Bathroom Mystery" as well as a novel I threw in the trash the next year; to my seventh and ninth grade teacher Ms. Shallenberger who told me I had great potential; for my eight grade teacher who made me take on the role of Anne in The Diary of Anne Frank; for my tenth grade teacher Ms. Evans who encouraged me to try poetry and helping me discover I liked it; for my choir teacher Ms. Eisenhauer and my drama teacher Ms. Somers who both taught me that pretending to be courageous on stage and actually being courageous on stage are nearly the same thing. For coaches who helped me find new ways to shine; if I couldn't get faster than first string JV 100m dash,

I could go out for shot put and discus throwing and do well. For college professors who expected "more" of my writing and who graded me accordingly – you challenged me and forced me to grow. For pastors and Christian mentors who encouraged and taught me in faith. For this great cloud of witnesses to creativity and encouragement in my life – I can't thank you enough. I hope I can encourage others like you have all encouraged me.

9 781735 769561